MOONLIGHTER

Johnny Walton

Moonlighter

1ˢᵗ Edition
POD

KBR
Petrópolis
2013

Publisher **Noga Sklar**
Text Edition **KBR**
Cover **KBR (Google Image)**

ISBN: 978-85-8180-176-6

KBR Editora Digital Ltda.
www.kbrdigital.com
www.facebook.com/kbrdigital
atendimento@kbrdigital.com.br
55|24|2222.3491

FIC043000 - Fiction

Printed in USA

Johnny Walton has been in the U.S. Navy for nearly a decade. He wrote *Moonlighter* while underway on the submarine USS RHODE ISLAND. He currently lives on his sailboat in Charleston, SC, where he continues to write and drink like a sailor.

Email: thejohnnyfanclub186282@yahoo.com

TABLE OF CONTENTS

CHAPTER 1

Who You Are

The image you project to others cannot just be what you want to be—it can, I guess, but not if you want what I think you want. It has to be a balance between what you should ideally be, and a little bit of what they want to be themselves. 'They' can be people you want to know, people you should already know, people you know but with whom you are not in an inner circle etc.

Take two guys. Both are Physics majors who program computers for fun. They look the same, they both dress nerdy and they both started college as virgins. Imagine that, virgins! The difference is one has had numerous girlfriends by now, he makes more money and he actually gets invited to parties. The other stays in his dorm every weekend and plays video games with other guys who don't do anything for his social life, and he is still yet to kiss a girl. That is a true story. One was my first client; the other was his roommate and close friend when they began college. Needless to say, they are not so close anymore.

How? The answer is simple. The one who gets out made the decision to meet girls, and go to parties. People don't hate him because he is smart. Most college kids would kill for that kind of aptitude. He owns it. Of course, he needed a push, which I was happy to give him, but that was all it took. By not trying to change his clothes or lie about the kind of dude he was it was easier to feel in his own skin, and better about making friends with people who were completely different than him. Some of those people had opportunities and ideas and parents' companies with a need for a kid who had computer skills. Hence the more money. He got better summer jobs because he put himself out there. Sometimes that's all one has to do.

I was walking late to class. When I walk I keep my hands in my pockets and I swagger. I whistle and I wink, nod and acknowledge nearly everyone that I walk past, depending on my mood. I strike up conversations with people who look familiar and I meet new people all of the time. Because of this, I am almost never on time. I am also never alone on a Friday, Saturday or Sunday unless I choose to be.

The one exception to my late habit is when I meet with clients. I have a $700 watch to ensure that I am never late for them. A ten-dollar watch would do the trick, but I don't feel the obligation to follow through when I measure my punctuality with something plastic and made in China. It sends the wrong message to people who want to be like me, and for now, at the age of 21, barely getting by in college, my livelihood depends a little (a lot) on people wanting to be like me.

I was whistling (poorly) "Rock You like a Hurricane," when I was approached by someone I consider a leech. Not like the colloquial term for a loser. Not even like a metaphor, but a real parasite that takes time from me. I have spent years diplomatically trying to weed them out without ruining a certain amount of harmony that surrounds my situation.

I have a small group of friends who are decent enough. But they are too much like me. We meet in the course of my work very frequently. I don't think most of them really know what I do. It doesn't matter. I don't know what most of them do either. Call me distant. I have always been apathetic about the personal lives of those around me, and for a good reason: it doesn't really matter what they do and it doesn't matter if they know what I do. I don't talk about work and I don't listen when they do it. One works at a shoe store. What could he possibly say about his job that interests me?

Next are clients. Clients are first and foremost as far as my priorities go, but in my esteem they are below friends (in spite of what my day planner says) and above professors and girls. I also have a large group of followers, gutless suck-ups who dream about being like me. They bother me with news about inane things that mean nothing to me and things that are nothing more than a chance to initiate small talk. They stop me on my way to wherever to show me new jeans or man purses I don't care about. Worse yet, they talk about their lives. They talk about things like sunglasses and homework and the weather; also something I do not care much about. Actually, I do have some hang-ups about the weather, but not in such a way that I need some stranger to comment on it. Leeches.

I capitalize on a very basic human desire. I think what I do actually ties a few of them together, but what I do know is that everyone wants to fit in. Everyone wants sex and everyone wants to be seen with the other people who get a lot of those things in an effort to get even more. There is no end to the social dynamics of horny 20 year olds and there is no distance many won't go with mommy and daddy's cash. I am a student, barely, and a businessman. And to a degree, a prophet to some.

Most guys at my default four year university—let's be clear: this school was no-one's first choice—scrimp and work sub-menial after-school jobs trying to buy clothes for a certain self-image they have not fully developed. They hang out with people who in no way perpetuate that image and they always turn out like a 500 piece puzzle missing 300 pieces. I give them the hope of a few more pieces. . .for a reasonable price. Quid pro quo. I don't always ask for much, but then, I don't always have to do much.

Other clients spend the parental unit's money, and most of those guys come from a polytechnical institute within a reasonable driving distance. It is easily worth my time to meet up with numerous clients on a Sunday. Or Monday, for that matter. I don't often go to my classes and any day that works for them works for me. I like to keep my advice local, spend locally, and fuck locally. While thinking globally, of course. And recycling.

I kept walking. I passed the leech with a simple hurried hello and I continued to whistle my song. Most of the time those guys get the hint. I can say with much certainty that I don't really hate anyone. Whenever I smell one coming (read: leech) I do my best just to keep it short or ignore. I realized after some time that I don't know enough of that Benatar song to whistle it, so I changed to "Final Countdown." It would be another 5 minutes of whistling until I had the same realization about that song too. I have these epiphanies weekly.

I eventually got to where I was going and walked up to a locked door. Inside was a class to which I "belonged." However, Herr Professor, Professor Heine, had a locked-door policy. Once class starts, no one comes in. I pointed out on day one, one of the few days I made it on time, that if there were a fire we would all cook inside. I attribute my 40% in his class to his lack of understanding of my sense of humor. Also, as I would find out, locked doors can still be opened from the inside.

I'm sorry I'm not a locksmith. I just figured that instead of a stick up his ass, he kept a key.

He was a real motivator.

I honestly thought I was going to make it today. Oh well.

Since I was already late and academics were a lost cause I figured I would do what any 21 year old would do in my situation: I went to get a beer for breakfast. Paradise Café sold domestic drafts from 8am to 8pm and I could get eggs and a Bud for $5. Recession special.

What I loved most about Paradise Café was the me-time. In spite of its proximity to campus, and wide drinking window, it was full of geriatrics, so I was bound not to be bothered. I could sit and pretend to read the newspaper and people-watch all morning. I think it would be an ideal place at 2am for drunk college kids, but there was something about the atmosphere that kept the clientele old and wizened.

Old people are notoriously bad tippers. One left my waitress his dentures.

I walked in and she seated me at the corner table I sat in every time and watched how people interacted. There was not a vast array of humanity to learn from here, but it is where I had the idea in the first place to do what I do. I guess I still come here as an ode to my personal progress. My one rule for Paradise is that I do not study here. It is a place to come and do absolutely nothing. I rarely even bring friends.

My eggs came scrambled, the usual, my toast was wheat, and my beer was cold. Realistically I would normally be more apt to drink an Americano at this hour, but the coffee here was awful. It was diner quality and I hated it. Call me a snob, say what you will, but I think it is safer to drink motor oil than to consume too much diner coffee. So beer it was. I would eventually get my coffee fix when I met with James in a couple of hours. He wanted to get together at a coffee shop, so I could save my appetite for the black go-juice.

Chapter 2

Opportunity

When an opportunity presents its self you have two options: 1) do nothing, which most of the average fucks will choose to do or, 2) jump on it like a wolf on a deer. Period. If you cannot take what life gives you then there are plenty of bridges for you to march off of and take control for once of your life, at least for a second or two. Say yes to life.

There is a certain amount of chance and luck in the world. You cannot deny it. But what you can deny is your dependence on it. You cannot control everything, or even most things. But what you can control is when and where you will be to ensure that you hedge your bets well enough so that you raise your statistical chances for a certain amount of success.

If you want to meet more girls but do not have all kinds of time because of heavy schoolwork, do your homework in a coffee shop and make small talk with one a day. That adds up pretty quickly. If you work too much or that second job is killing your social life, apply for a second job that puts you in social situations. Restaurants, coffee shops, bookstores. Anything is fair game. But nothing in life is really fair. You have to make it fair, for you.

A friend of mine was disillusioned that he could not find the athletic types of girls as plentifully as he would have liked. So I recommended he work at a gym or a sporting goods store and after he made that 'career change' he met 30 girls of his dreams. Location location location.

I think it should have been 'itself' at the beginning, not 'its self.' I need to change that. I have sent my manuscript to three places and not one has cited my grammar. Damn. Also, should I call people fucks? I don't know. I need to think about it. I will probably do what I do with most of my great ideas and bounce it off of someone who is going to tell me how great it is, which is normally fine, because they are right. Unfortunately, when I listen to them I don't ever get that constructive advice that is going to make my goal more attainable. I have tried a few times to get this published and a few times they have yet to finish it or pursue it further. I copyrighted a few months ago so I could post some of its content in a few literary circles and ask for inputs. I mostly got shunned for what I had to say. I didn't realize how many girls were involved in those groups. Someone actually told me if I was trying to write the antithesis to the Bible that I need to change the name of the author.

I personally don't think it's all that bad. No, it's not Matthew, Mark, Luke or John. Or Job or Leviticus. But if those books were so full of good advice than maybe we need another Inquisition or some witch-hunts to root out people like me. I think it's the modern Ecclesiastes. Says right there in the original: two people to a bed.

It is almost 2pm. Pretty soon James is going to walk in. He is going to greet me and sit down for a cup of coffee. Specifically, a white chocolate mocha with an extra shot of espresso for me. It is already on its way. James is going to get himself a cup of something a little plainer, but good nonetheless and we are going to have a candid discourse; I am going to ask him what he has done this week and then he is going to pull out a notebook with a bunch of scribblings in it. It is going to contain notes on the progress he has made toward: 1) His fitness goal of running a marathon; 2) his anxiety about approaching girls; and 3) his aspirations of designing video games.

After I look over his dossier of life and living, we are going to shoot the shit and I am inevitably going to give him some words of wisdom, some ideas and some insight about how much progress he is making. Most of which are going to come off the top of my head and some of which I actually believe.

I don't like running. I don't play video games and I can't relate to the thing about not talking to girls, but what I have that James wants is answers. I simply told him to do the things that he wanted to do and he appreciates the motivation. If you tell someone "do what you want", nothing is going to happen. If you tell someone who wants to be a runner but who just cannot motivate himself 'go for a run today' he will do it. That is why I meet with these guys. James has run a half marathon, gotten five phone numbers (one was real) and began designing his own video game thanks to yours truly.

He does this stuff because I tell him to. He listens because he pays me. He pays me because he needed guidance, and it is too expensive when it comes from life coaches, it is boring when it comes from churches and it is almost always wrong when you get it from friends. I am none of those things; I am The Devil's Advocate. So to speak.

James is about one of 80 people that I have 'helped.' I have been doing this for two years and I am finally gaining momentum. He and several others like him give me about 50 to 100 dollars a week for my advice. They like my outside-of-the-box thinking. I come off as having a tailored plan, and after getting a couple of nerds laid, I got a pretty good reputation for my help. The getting laid part is always the lowest common denominator. The running and the video games thing are tertiary to him compared to my ability to help him get laid, but it is a good cover for him to act more like he just wanted some type of life coaching.

As I sat alone at my table, gleaning over my manuscript and thinking about what I had planned for James I caught the attention of a familiar face. She was a brunette I could not place to save my life. I smiled and she smiled but quickly looked away. Shy. Well, my shy brunette, this is your lucky day.

I leaned over; I don't think it made a real difference in our six feet apart. "I have to tell you the truth, which I don't normally do to pretty girls," I smiled my most million-dollar smile. "I recognize you from somewhere, but I just can't put my finger on it."

"We were in the same biology class freshman year." Look at the memory on that one.

"Oh man, now I have to be embarrassed about my bad mammary *and* that you saw me attempt a science class." Another million-dollar smile. A smile back from her. This is too easy if you just make it too easy. It's a wonder I cannot get my book published. I'm so good at so many things.

"I take it you've moved on from science. Maybe towards, say, psychology?"

"Good job, you can see the book on my table." She laughed.

"Look, I don't want to keep you from your schoolwork or anything, and I definitely don't want to cut you off when my 'associate' shows up, but maybe we can keep in touch? I would love to hear more about," I squinted and stared at her book, "*Early Child Development: Infancy to Pre-Teens.*" I jotted down, and handed her my number. She gave me hers and I was going to sleep with her in about one week.

I tell my guys never to give their number out. If they think it is okay they overdo it and look sorry giving it away. I break my own rules plenty because at this stage of the game I don't look at this as a challenge or a competition. It is more like a transaction between adults who want the same thing. She wants to make me happy, and I want her to make me happy. I just need to give her a chance.

My reputation for my work is not too much more than whispers and passed down phone numbers exchanged between friends. I work off of referrals. Most girls as well as much of the general male population do not know exactly what I do, but I am always seen with new followers. Intuitive people think I have something really great going for me, which I do, and others just think I am that cool, which I am.

I have a full schedule. I make a lot of phone calls, I check up on people, I meet for breakfast, lunch and dinner and everything in between. This leaves no real time to be a good (real) friend and consumes just enough of my time that I cannot really excel in school, much to the chagrin of every adult figure in my life. However, without my work I would be scraping by, living off loans and eating ramen for a history degree. If that is success then I am happy being unsuccessful.

CHAPTER 3

To whom it may concern,

After a careful review of the material you submitted, we regret to inform you that neither the subject matter, nor the actual contents fit within the guidelines and standards to which we publish.

If you have any questions about the review process feel free to visit our website, or view our submission guidelines on the FAQs page.

Good luck in your future endeavors and we hope to hear from you again.

Sheryl Smith-Rivera
Editor, Westward Publishers

The publishing process is elusive. I am used to being good at everything I do. I actually keep the book a secret, more or less, because I don't want people to ask me in six months why I haven't published. I cannot look like a failure in any facet of my life. That is bad business when people turn to you for success. And most of the time it feels like there is a very real chance that I will not be able to publish. I don't know how many tries it is going to require, but I am up to three.

The last publisher who declined my book said I had too many incomplete ideas. This one didn't say shit. Who reads submission guidelines? I sure as hell never considered something like that. I am not to the point where I would hire an agent, but some say it is the only way to go. It all comes down to the fact that I really just need to sleep with the right person. How many girls have got to where they were going because the right bed opened up along the way? Why can't that opportunity be extended to me? Why can't a guy fuck his way to the top? Wouldn't that show the world that we have finally come around? Maybe I am just too progressive for this generation.

In spite of my inability to publish, I still think I give pretty valid advice. I know it works because people come back to me, and I can watch them transform their social lives. I have objective evidence. Not that 100 percent of my advice is perfect. I have dropped the ball a few times. I have made a few things up on the fly and had them backfire. Fortunately, anything I think of gets field tested on people who are less cool, so if it works I know that I have gold. If not, then we all understand that someone who was not so cool couldn't pull off advice on how to fit in. We move on.

It is not always so simple, though. I have had some guys fail on me who would not own it. Those few, isolated incidents came with a barrage of hate email, phone calls and in-person Fuck Yous. But still, no one spreads bad press because no college student wants to admit that he paid me for help on how to be cool and I fucked it up. It would make him look like a douche and I would still get off scot-free, because I actually do get laid and people know it. I can imagine that my business would suffer a bit from it, but the beauty of an adolescent's desperation is that desperation can and does easily overcome the good judgment of one's peers and I would venture to say that with one success story and twelve failures I could still get clients.

I looked down at my coffee and then up at the barista. I didn't recognize her that well and had I not just gotten, wait a sec—I had to look down at it—Laura's phone number, I would probably be getting this girl's right now. She was tall. Maybe an inch or two taller than I, but manageable. I like slender girls and she fit the bill. Laura won't be here next time.

James walked in at 1:57. He nodded to me and made his way over to the barista. Before the door fully closed she walked in too. *She* walked in. I didn't know who she was but she was certainly something else. She was legs that you would not believe. She was blonde hair that blondes get jealous of. She was a smile, a grin full of white teeth that said "if you make it into my bed, I am going to do some very bad things to you." I watched her long legs walk to the barista and she whispered something to. . .James?! Holy Shit.

He looked over his shoulder, motioned towards me and she walked over.

"So you're the guy?"

I liked her voice too. I wanted to play it cool, but I was still in shock that she was here with him. How the hell did he get her? I must be better at this than I thought. I immediately fell back on instinct.

"Yeah." I leaned back in my chair and extended a hand. We shook and she sat. James walked over with two coffees and put them down. I stood up and shook his hand.

"I see you met Chase." As in 'don't try chasing me, I am dating a nerd.' He was trying not to gloat that he landed a 10.

"Yep." I was still monosyllabic but I could feel it wearing off.

"It's nice to finally meet you, Tristan. James talks about you all the time." I was glad she knew my name already, so I could enjoy 15 extra seconds of shock. I just pretended to be coy. It was cute. Most of the time girls like it.

Also, on a side note, yes, my name is Tristan. I was named after some German freedom fighter or myth or something. I still don't know why every Tristan I met growing up was a girl. It is a guy's name. All anyone knows about my name is some band nerds made Wagner jokes and every girl I meet brings up Brad Pitt in "Legends of the Fall," or a girlfriend of hers with the same name. I wish I could have just capitalized on Legends of the Fall thing.

James introduced me as his buddy. I never told anyone

that I had clients or even alluded to what I do for them. As far as she knew, I was like a big brother to this guy. He wasn't totally secretive with her, though. She seemed to know that I was a little more than a 'cool friend.' I don't know what she knew.

"What do you do, Chase?"

"I'm a computer programmer. I work for an internet provider."

I tried to keep her talking. I needed to find a chink in that gorgeous armor. Since he brought her along this was not a meeting about him, or his progress. It was for him to showboat his hot blonde. So I didn't feel bad for focusing the conversation on her. She likes old films, rocky road and gave off a family(ish) vibe without ever talking about family. She seemed religious but spared me the Jesus talk, and she did charity work every week for a year because of a new year's resolution. I liked the resolve. I think it could have gone towards something more productive than after school programs, but I liked her nonetheless. She was aesthetic to look at and fun to listen to. Not too many girls have that problem. That is, the latter.

"It was kind of funny," she went on, "James was in our office applying for a temp position and just asked me out point blank." They looked at each other and smiled. I taught him point blank. It was mine. It works too. I recommend trying it somewhere you don't normally go. If she says no, oh well. If she says yes, you have a date. Easy. No lead up, no preparation, no sweat.

"I mean, how could I say no? It takes a lot of guts." James was pretty proud of himself as she sat there talking about it. I could see it in his eyes. "He told me that he is training for a marathon and I run too, so. . ."

It was I who encouraged him to run. It was I who encouraged him to do everything and *he* was sitting there with the new girl of my dreams. Bastard.

There was a lot more small talk and I was determined to get that girl. That's all there was to it. We all finished our coffee and the small talk and then stood up to leave.

"You know, Chase," I held them up for a moment longer

"I was thinking about getting a new computer myself, and could use the expert opinion. . .It wouldn't be too much of a bother if I called you at work for a little bit of free advice?"

I looked at James and smiled. He smiled back; disarmed.

"Here." She handed me a card.

Chase Anderson
Cyber-whatever company
555-blablah (I don't remember off the top of my head).

"Perfect. Let's all get out of here. We have busy lives." As they walked out, I followed, but not too close behind. I said goodbye and James shut the door behind him. I made sure Laura was not looking over and walked up to the counter.

To the girl at the counter: "Hey, can I ask you something?"

"Sure." She was a strong 7. Maybe 7.5, but completely respectable.

"When do you work again? Because I want to come by later this week and get your phone number. Now isn't so good for me." I glanced over at Laura.

"I'm engaged." She showed me her hand. Yep. Engaged.

"Well then, thanks for the coffee."

CHAPTER 4

Amelioration

There is something very distinct about people who are better. They are, to put it simply, better. Anyone can dress up nice. Anyone can get new cologne. A guy can get a $65 haircut and he can polish his shoes. Women and other guys, your competition, can smell the fake a mile away. It is in the sound of your voice. It is in your demeanor and it comes out of your pores. So instead of acting like you are a great guy, just be one. Instead of acting like someone with good style, get better style.

The secret to being better is to just to do it. The object is to stay 'true' to yourself, whatever that means, while accruing skills, knowledge and things that others want. The way it works is when you know a lot about something that is interesting to everyone, no one cares when you don't know about the television show they were talking about. But if you talk about some television program and don't know anything about the current events they are interested in, you look like a dumbass. None of that requires changing much about your mind. Just a change of mindset, really.

Having dinner with Dustin was a treat. Mainly because if I had real friends I would want them to be like him. He was actually a decent guy, who could hold a conversation. We knew each other before he started paying me for my insight. He was the kind of dude who had shelves full of 'teach yourself' books. He just wanted to be good at everything, almost to a fault.

So, no, he didn't need me the way the other guys needed me, I was just another project for his brain, with one, glaring exception: he needed to be much better with girls. It was not that he was incapable and I needed to fix him. It was that he came off as too smart, too arrogant, I guess. So, in a way, he *did* need me the way other guys do, but he wasn't afraid to admit the real reason. That is what made him different.

He lived on campus too, so we agreed to meet at Angie's. It was about a block away and had the most excellent veggie pizzas. Also, I like walking there. The shortest route there was past all of the frat houses. Not that I liked frats or the people in them, but the houses were all super old and really cool. But the best part was that in the Fall (it was Fall at the time), the leaves of all of the old trees would cover the sidewalk, the lawns, the street and the roofs of the houses. Of course, after the pledges started rushing, that was the first thing to go. Those poor bastards would be out there, rain or shine, raking leaves until not a single one was to be found. No matter what the frat or sorority. Raking leaves. Friends in other schools never did such things. I guess that was our thing.

I was taking my time, strolling along, when I heard my name. The familiar voice was enough to make me want to ignore it and continue on. But what I could not ignore was the voice running over to intercept me.

Now it is time to discuss what a 'leech' is. My definition is someone who insists on talking to me longer than the 30 seconds it takes to establish a chatty, friendly rapport. After that time they are parasites who are trying to suck the time, insight or association out of me without so much as a thanks or a reach around. A friend is someone I want to be around (kind of). A client is someone who wants to be around me and sees to it that it is worth my time. A leech is someone who interrupts me on my way to one or the other. Most of the time they piss me off. Other times I let it sink in that people actually benefit from being seen with me.

"Hey Tristan! What brings you out here?" He did a kind

of half-assed jog to catch up to me. This time, it just pissed me off.

"Well, I was thinking about rushing your frat, but I didn't go to the Greek meeting last week."

I tried to sound as convincing as possible. It was well known, my stance on fraternities: ANTI.

"You know, I could talk to Phillip for you, I'm sure the guys would"—I didn't even know who Phillip was. I was sure that I did not like him, though.

"I'm kidding, man." I saw the hope shatter like crystal. "Actually I am going to dinner." Shit! Did that sound like an invite? I hope not.

"If you want, Tristan, you should stop by sometime and . . ."

"Look, I would love to talk, but I got to cut you off, man," man as in I-have-no-idea-what-your-name-is. "I am already late and I need to get back and study." I looked at my watch for added urgency.

Silence him, Tristan. Neutralize the time vampire. Walk. Away. Now.

I just kept walking. He stood there staring at me, watching me walk away. I knew that he was watching and thinking to himself that he liked my (blank). Insert piece of clothing, accessory, my hair, my something. No, I may not have known his name, but I think I knew him. And I definitely know his kind. He was going to walk a little more like I do tomorrow, or he was going to get a watch this weekend. I put a cigarette in my lips and lit it. I don't chain smoke, but I love the occasional stick. I would have bet at the time that my frat friend would be a smoker by the end of the week after seeing me do it.

Some people call me arrogant. It is an assumption they make because I am confident. Why should I be shy about my style, or my ability to communicate well and make others want to be like me? In college, athletes get trophies when they win. I don't win games, I win a much older competition called sexual selection.

I was almost to Angie's when I walked past a couple of freshmen talking. One was easily a 9. The other was a 7 who could probably dress herself up to an 8 if she tried. They both looked at me. I looked back, smiled and sized up the 9 from head to toe with an innocent smile. She looked away and started to blush. I have a feeling I am going to see her again. I also think it is going to go very well for the two of us.

I opened the door and Dustin was in a booth reading the *Brothers Karamazov*. I was secretly jealous of the guy for exuding so much intelligence. We both looked out of the window where the two freshmen were. The 9 situated herself to look at the window in which I sat. I stopped being jealous of Dustin.

"How? I just don't get how." He really didn't.

"You know I was a virgin until I came to college?" I tell anecdotes like that so that guys know it is possible to change. If they think that I was always cool then it seems like I just have a cool pheromone and they won't pay me for any advice. Except that virgin thing was true. My high school girlfriend wouldn't go past the hand job. She had another relationship with Jesus, which made it impossible to go round third.

"Then how did you make the turnaround? 0 to 100 in a year, two years?"

"How many parties have you gone to this week? You have a shitload of friends. If you are around more girls and more people in general, your odds are better." That was all there was to it. I think he still had some baggage from a pretty bad break-up with this really average girl. I knew him before he came to me for help. I didn't charge him what I charged everyone else. I really wanted to help.

"I went to two, and they sucked."

"No, man, *you* sucked." Man as in 'friend', not man as in 'I forgot your name.'

"There were these stupid, drunk 18 year olds everywhere, I'm not like that. I just. . ." He looked over, our pizza came. He knew my favorite and ordered it before I got there. What an angel.

"Anything else for you two?" Our server was cute.

"Coke, please."

"And for you?" She looked at Dustin.

"I don't do the hard stuff anymore, just gimme a tea, easy on the ice." She smiled at him and then off she went for the drinks.

"Your homework this week is easy, Dustin."

"Oh God. What are you scheming?"

"Just ask her out. 'Will you come with me to a party this weekend?'"

"What if she says no? It would completely ruin this place for me."

"Look at her." I motioned towards a mildly good-looking girl serving a pizza at another table. "She cried and threw something at my car when we broke up. We didn't even really break up, I just told her that I was seeing someone else after we had sex. It's not awkward now. This is a pizza joint. I come here for pizza. It's not dramatic."

"Okay, fine. If she says no, you pay for the pizza."

"Deal."

We spent the rest of the meal talking about my approach. I was not a certified life coach. I don't have some magic method. I just make up what sounds good and go with it. I always thought others would benefit from taking my lead. Sometimes my advice is off. Rarely. Even bad advice puts people into the game, and for some, it is more of a numbers game. Bad approaches work too. Sometimes, on the right—or wrong, rather—kind of girls. One thing I am not is a therapist. I cannot deal with issues and when he tried talking about his breakup I would always change the subject. There are people way more qualified to talk to him about that than this guy.

That waitress, the one that I told him I slept with. That never happened. I needed to tell him something to shut him up with all of his speculating. He could probably speculate a girl right out of his bed.

Today was not the day for serious coaching, or advocating. It really didn't matter what I called it. It was the same when all of the pretenses are taken out of the equation. Dustin just chatted in general terms and didn't ask. I didn't contribute much more than the waitress bet and we ate the whole pizza. I left him with some very specific advice about his posture, and aside from chastising him for not going out more, I didn't do much for Dustin that night. He put off asking until the very end.

After she said yes, I had to admit something to him.

"I was actually nervous for you." I told the proud client.

"Why is that? Am I that much of a long shot?"

"No, I just realized that I forgot my wallet, and couldn't afford to lose that bet tonight."

CHAPTER 5

Tristan,

Fuck you. There are not many people I hate on this campus, but you are certainly one of them.

I paid you for help that you did not actually provide. I spent four textbooks worth of cash on something that I could have looked up online and none of it even worked. I think there are some serious flaws in your business practice and if I ever see you again I am going to kick your ass.

You are a liar and a thief and I hope you burn in hell.

In spite of the grave threat I knew this kid well, and I had nothing to fear. As I said before, I do have a few detractors, but as time goes by they become fewer and further between. This guy in particular was a hard case who could not grasp anything I tried to drill into his oversized brain. I hate nerds to no end, and this job has taught me two lifetimes worth of patience, but the facts are that people with incredibly high IQs don't like listening to people who don't get good grades. Apparently, people with even more incredibly high IQs won't even listen to people that they pay to teach them.

I had a hard time taking this one personally and I filed it away in my folder labeled HATE. It wasn't the biggest folder in my email, but it certainly was not the smallest either. I had a good laugh to myself, but lamented that there was no one that I could really tell this story to. I didn't have anyone who I let into this circle of my life. The first thing that would happen is that he would try to capitalize on my idea and include himself. I say 'he' and 'him' because I think I am physically incapable of letting women close. There are over a million things I would do with them that I absolutely would not do with a guy, but sharing my ideas and opening up are not among them.

I had the afternoon off in terms of school because I decided to take a furlough day, and since the weather was still nice enough to eat lunch in the open air I called Jeremy R. Ainslie, one of about three actual friends of mine. He was also free and we were going to meet up at Habana Banana. In spite of its awful name, it had the best empanadas. H.B., as I call it, to avoid sounding like a seven year old, was a little Cuban place where one eats on the patio in plain sight of a C food rating sign. I think the old Cuban who opened the place thought it stood for Cuba or Castro. I figured it stood for 'the inspector was pissed off that he didn't speak English and gave him a C'. Or it had something to do with the two dogs that were allowed anywhere in the place, including the kitchen. Either way, empanadas=great.

I was in a particularly good mood today and was starving for some Cuban. I also wanted one of the Cubans or Dominicans who worked there and was determined to overcome the cultural barrier—the one where most immigrants don't let their children have one night stands with whites. That wasn't my top priority, but she was on my to-do list.

When I showed up, I saw a very dismayed Jeremy and didn't want to ask. I didn't want him to talk about his feelings and I didn't want to be a shoulder to cry on. I wasn't that kind of friend. Not for free. I usually don't let my clients talk too much about their feelings unless it is completely relevant to what we are working through. Most of the time it is not, so I don't have to hear it.

"What's the matter, Sad Face?"

My desire not to talk about it was completely overcome by my desire to make fun of him.

"Yesterday. . ." he paused too long. I could see that it was for effect, but after about three seconds the effect wore off and I stopped caring about his drama ". . .I was almost sexually assaulted."

Now I'm interested. "What do you mean?"

"I was at the lake the other day."

We live about thirty minutes from a lake where kids go to party and fuck and, as I would soon find out, pick up trash.

"There was a newspaper on the ground close to where I was sitting. I was by the water just reading, since Amber is out of town"

He was kind of a pussy about his girlfriend, but she was super hot and she fit in well, so no one really cared that Jeremy was practically married. What did kind of bother me is that he went to go read in the shade by a lake when his girl was out of town.

"So I picked it up and threw it away. It was no big deal, but this dude walked up. He was about twice my age and seemed a little weird. He told me that he thought it was cool that I picked up trash and that most people nowadays would have just left it."

"And that's when he raped you. Your just reward for all that philanthropy, Jeremy."

"Philanthropy is when you help people. I *know* you don't know anything about that, T. So this dude was kind of weird and tried to keep the conversation going. It seemed forced, almost. Every time I tried to make my exit he kept talking. Then his phone rang. He looked at it, casually said 'It's the parents, I'll talk to them later.' And hit ignore.

"I figured this guy lived with them and that he was a little slow or something. I mean, why the hell would he try so hard to keep the conversation going, you know? He obviously needed a friend or someone to hang out with, or something. Right? At least all signs point to no friends."

"All signs point to raping you."

"I was just being nice and chatting, trying to get out of there and he asked if I lived around there. I said no, I live near the university, and he does too.

"You're telling me that we have a rapist in our midst?"

"I started to walk to my car and he walked with me. Just talking the whole time. At first, I did that thing that normal adults do and related to him, but after a while I was giving yes/no answers, still walking away. It must have been like thirty minutes of him talking."

"I think that was a good idea."

"What?"

"Relating to him early on." I said. "Most rapists dehumanize their victims so the fact that you were making yourself more of a person is probably the reason you are alive today."

"Fuck you, Tristan." That was the second time I heard that today. If my email earlier counted as hearing. "I could just see that this dude was lonely. Then he asked me if I wanted to grab a beer sometime. I kind of froze up, and said, sure. I flake out on plans all the time, so there was no reason I couldn't this time, right?

"The next words out of his mouth are 'How's tomorrow?' I mean, fuck dude. Most people hide the fact that they are lonely and just meet people online. Whatever, so I said sure again and we arranged to get a beer in town. It was like a block from my place so I could just walk over, have a beer and make my exit."

"He raped you at your place then? Seriously fucked up."

"I met him at that sports bar, the one on Arbor Street. I never go there so if I was seen doing charity work it wouldn't make a difference."

"Philanthropy, you mean?"

"Eat a dick. So it was the same thing all over again. I sat there and he just kept talking. It was all small talk, nothing interesting or relevant. Then it kind of turned into twenty questions. He kept staring off into space and thinking, before he would ask me the next question."

"He was fantasizing about you tied to the radiator in some basement."

"I couldn't really take it anymore. I finished my beer, said thanks and got up to leave. He followed me outside and asked when we could do this again. I told him I don't know, and kept walking. He asked me if he could ask me something."

"He asked to rape you?"

"He asked if I was gay."

"So," I returned the favor of that excruciatingly long pause earlier. More pause. Okay, good enough. "You went on a gay date."

"It wasn't a date."

"You met for drinks. When I meet a girl for drinks it is called a date."

"Well, if she doesn't sleep with you, do you still call it a date?"

"Yeah, it's just a bad date." I leaned over our table, put my hands on his shoulders, and looked at him with as much gravity as I could muster. "We're just glad you're still alive, son."

"A gay date. God damn it."

"Don't worry, man."

"Should I tell Amber?"

"No way. When the cat is away, the mice will play. She doesn't want to know that you strayed. As long as you are there for her when she get back."

The Cuban girl was not even there today, so I settled for empanadas and making fun of Jeremy.

CHAPTER 6

Focus

Sometimes you may have to give your attention to something you don't want to give it to. You may have to give your time to something or someone who does not seem to deserve it. But, no matter how fair it seems in the finiteness of your life, you will have to do it, and if you can do it with a smile and with a genuine sense of focus, you will come out on top.

Siddhartha was not a businessman. He was a starving, ascetic monk when he decided to drop all of that and learn about love. He met a beautiful woman who agreed to teach him, but she had some prerequisites; she did not tell him to practice lovemaking. She did not tell him to work out and become chiseled, she told him to become rich. So he went to work and became rich.

It was a small matter of time before he was banging the hell out of her. All thanks to his ability to keep his goals in line with his priorities. So focus, become rich and get the girl.

I don't like to use fictional anecdotes, but this one summed up my point so well. It didn't require a shit-load of elaboration or explanation. I think that is the beauty of *Siddhartha*. Unfortunately, I could not go overboard with references to the same book; I thank my 10th grade English teacher for forcing that down my throat. I never really read and the three books I can actually reference are *Siddhartha*, which I read four years ago, The Bible, which I read excerpts of in Bible class when I was eight, and my book, which is a modern Bible for the young bachelor.

I was sitting at my desk, feet up, thumbing through my mail when my cell phone rang.

"Hello, Taylor." It was 7:30pm. Taylor: 30 min, according to my day planner.

"Hey, Tristan."

Taylor was okay, I guess. He was shy, maybe a little awkward. He didn't like talking to me in person because he felt like less of a man for asking for my advice. The age-old tradition of asking dad was long dead. I think the free love of the 70's made his advice ineffective for our generation of texting, MTV2-watching party-girls who need certain illusions before jumping into bed. It is nothing over the top, but they don't want to feel accountable. They have to justify it in 10 years when they are married with kids. It's not free love. It's cheap love.

"Taylor, you went out with that girl last week, tell me what happened."

"Ah, it was great. We ended up going for a coffee."

"What kind of stuff did you talk about?" This was my litmus test.

"Her family, growing up, her major."

"Hold on, you talked about school?" I always thought it was a bad idea to spend too much time on something she is going to willingly talk about for hours. No matter how long she talks about her major, it does not mean she is interested in you. It means she can talk about herself, misleading thousands of guys across the country, every weekend, who think that their date was hunky dory because it lasted forever. Wrong.

"No, man, it's cool, she is studying English and my grandpa knew William Faulkner. It was the perfect segue."

I really didn't give a damn about William Faulkner, and I didn't care how it applied to the conversation.

"Segue to what?"

"To the book I am writing." I think he told me about it before. It was a long time ago and if I remember correctly it was boring, but I was beginning to approve of his conduct.

"So I took her back to my apartment to show her the manuscript. She said she didn't believe me, but she was smiling. I knew it was an invitation to something."

He really was getting a clue. I sat there, listening, staring at the shoes on my feet. I could never really focus on just the phone call. I was never one of those guys that came off like a material girl, but I do own about 20 pairs of shoes. It was a pair for every conceivable outfit I had. My secret to not being a Diva (and any guy with more than 15 pairs of shoes is usually a Diva) is to know what looks good ahead of time and just put it on. I do not require 45 minutes to get ready. Divas of either gender take forever to get ready for a night out. A guy grabs something, and puts it on. A smart guy grabs something that looks good and just puts it on.

Taylor continued. "And I showed her the stack of note-book paper and thumbed through it for her. I even showed her one of my favorite chapters, but I told her what you said."

"Oh yeah?" I totally forgot what I told him to say.

"Yeah, that if she wanted to see more I had to know her, and trust her. I told her that she had a lot of trust to build with me."

"And of course you were up all night screwing."

"No, we just made out. But the point is I really like her."

I help guys become slightly cooler, they get a chick, they fall in love and they are not cool anymore. They are barely confident, they give up on everything else because of one girl and they stop paying me for help because she was sooooo awesome that it was the end of the line.

"Taylor, do you remember what else we talked about?"

"Yeah, man, but she is awesome."

"If you are not going to marry her next month, if she is not absolutely the one, then you will be in the same boat you were in a month ago after she breaks up with you."

I was right. I bullshit too much for my own good, but I was right.

"What makes you so positive that we are going to break

up soon?" He was resisting reason. In my line of business we call that 'unwilling'. By 'we', I mean 'me', the one-man show.

"Because, Taylor, you are 20, she is 20. Both of you have two more years walking around a campus with 5000 potential girlfriends, boyfriends, mates, fuck-buddies, one-night-stands, accidents, casual hookups and every single other relationship you could imagine."

I have said this piece about 25 times now and I have saved about nine souls with it. Nine willing to listen. It was not going to be my fault if he gave up on life because he got to second base. I would, however, lose some cash flow.

As he tried justifying himself, I went back to looking at my mail, not really paying too much attention.

Something from school. Hmmm. I opened it. I was being kicked out of film class. I didn't know they could do that. I thought I had to assault someone or do heroin in the middle of class to actually lose my spot. The only rule I broke was not going. Weird. Shocking. It occurred to me that my standing was not that great in the first place and I didn't know where that left me academically.

"Fuck! Taylor, man, I gotta call you back, something just came up." I cut him off from some inane feelings-talk about some seven who was going to rip his heart out. I think this was a favor not letting him justify this any longer.

"Yeah, Tristan. Tomorrow okay?"

"Sure, I will email you the specifics." Click.

I read it again. There was a little more to it than just film. I was one year from graduation. This dropped elective was going to fuck up my summer in a big way. I had to figure something out. My life just became a Brady Bunch episode with a timeline, a speed bump, and a lesson to be learned. If only I could have a bake sale or win the solution on a radio show.

I sat there for a few minutes, reeling from the fumes of Taylor's idiocy, wallowing in my own and needing a plan.

When I am under pressure, I thrive. But before I can thrive, I need to go through a rough, 12-hour period of lots of pacing, worrying, jotting notes to myself and avoiding everyone.

I was so fucked.

CHAPTER 7

Hurdles

Also called brick walls, hiccups, and obstacles. You cannot foresee them, stop them or jump over them at times. I say, and I mean it, you can go around them. Not all the time, but sometimes the easy way out is what you want. If you are reading this, maybe all of those other books have failed you. The books that tell you to confront your problems. Those are a dime a dozen and if the advice in them were so easy and ubiquitous, then it would not have to be written so much, so many times. It would be more obvious.

Maybe, just maybe, in your professional life some of that stuff applies. Maybe you have to take the high road in your academic career. But your social life cannot be a series of high roads. It cannot be a complicated series of lies either, but the high road takes quite a bit of emotional scaffolding to construct and after one or two, they become exponentially harder to navigate.

I had this theory that most self-help books were written without one's wellbeing in sight because the people who write them write five or six, not one. If the first book was going to solve your problems, then why the hell do you need the whole series? If not, why the hell would you buy it?

I spent a good deal of time considering my own problem. This was kind of ironic for me because everyone knew me as the intuitive solution guy. You tell me your problem and I can spit out a reasonable course of action faster than you can say 'reasonable course of action.'

I concluded, very unfortunately, that I needed to bring up my GPA. There was going to be no easy way out of this one. If I could pull all Bs this semester, my GPA would be adequate to graduate. I had mostly Bs anyhow; as I said, medium quality university. I was almost fine, with two exceptions. One of which was film, which I did not have to worry about anymore. And the second was some intro to poli-sci. It was a history related elective that was so immensely hard to show up to I originally opted for the F. Until now. The class was not an attendance based grade, it was half homework, half final. I still had about a 60 percent the fall quarter to do some homework and ace the final, which would get me a B overall. Doing homework meant showing up to turn it in. Showing up meant waking up before 7am on Mondays, Wednesdays, and Fridays.

My future was looking bad. It was dark. Not 'fail out of school and starve on the streets' dark, but 'wake up at 6:30 on Mondays, Wednesdays, and Fridays' dark. I needed a pick-me-up. I didn't have to meet with, or talk to a client for about two more days, and I made no other plans, so I decided to cash in on that number I got from Chase. But first I needed to warm up. I reached into my wallet.

"Hello, Laura." The brunette that I met a couple of days before.

I dialed and it went to voicemail. I left a quick, upbeat message explaining that there was a party this weekend that she might enjoy and if she wasn't too busy reading books about children's brains that I would have more fun getting to know her than doing the usual party thing. I didn't know at that point if I was being ignored or having to play bullshit games. I can tell you either way that it did not matter one bit to me. There are too many yes's in the world to cry over the no's.

I looked at Chase's card. Then I dialed and immediately began hoping that she would not answer. I didn't know why, exactly, but I recalled that she did leave me a little speechless when we first met. I don't lose my cool because of pretty girls. I think it was that she was there with James. Whatever. It didn't matter now. The phone was ringing.

Three rings and a "Hello?" It was a dude. No, not a dude, a nerd. I hate nerds. Except the nerds that pay me.

"Hi, is Chase there?"

"Yes Sir, one moment." God, I hate nerds. Except Chase.

"This is Chase."

"Hey, it's me, Tristan?" I think I just said that as a question. It was either that or choke on the frog in my throat.

"Yeah, I remember. How goes?"

"I'm fine. I was thinking about getting that computer soon. And like I said before, I could really use some help."

She started laughing. "I must say, Tristan, I thought you were just trying to get my phone number. I never saw you as a computer guy."

"Oh yeah. I'm really not, but it's for school. . ." I thought for a second. "And stuff." I added stuff in lieu of social networking, porn and emailing clients (like your boyfriend) advice on getting girls. "Anyhow," I went on, "if we could meet up at (blah) computer warehouse I will buy you lunch in return for your professional opinion."

I didn't know what I was doing. I needed this girl. Unfortunately, it was going to cost me $800.

"Sure," she said. "I can take a long lunch on Friday."

Friday was two days from now and perfectly okay with me.

"Great, Friday. Say 11am?"

"Yeah, great. See you then, Tristan."

You may be wondering why I am not worried about hurting James. That is a great question. Since I am trying to be more academic so I don't fail out of school, let me share a historic quote with you. Thomas Jefferson once said: "Were all men to live their lives based on feelings alone, America would be nothing more than some idea, an entry in some pussy's diary." I don't actually think that is a real quote, but it would take so long to disprove that I think we can table the validity discussion for later.

He was paying me to teach him social skills, charm and confidence, not ethics. If I have given him a lifetime of knowledge and he has paid me for a couple of months advice, I think it's a pretty goddamn good trade-off. She is only taking me computer shopping, anyways.

Maybe I just want to be around someone who sees me as I am. I am allowed to like it that she doesn't see me as a few easy payments of 74.99 as a means of being popular. She was just going to help me buy a computer. I would almost consider that friendship.

I have done similar things before and had them happen to me. It's all a part of this big picture. James was not her soul mate and if they are not both in a legally protected institution (e.g. marriage), then I could reasonably compete with and get her without violating any ethical principle. I leave married chicks alone. Even engaged baristas. But I don't put friends above something we all know is more important. The only difference between me and what one would think is an ethical guy is I do the things I do and I stand behind them. Other guys do the things I do and in the next breath condemn people who do them.

In the end, people like me always win, and all of the little guys below us hold us up, work for us, hate us and make us rich.

I sleep at night.

CHAPTER 8

The Different Layers

Most guys who are successful with girls are also successful in the other aspects of their lives. It's not always true, but there are exceptions to every rule. This is one case where you do not benefit from being one.

Looks will only get you so far. The guys I help are almost always great at some things. Some of them are awesome at their hobbies or jobs. That is exactly what you need to be able to say when she asks about work. You are good at it. School? Also good at it. Your hobbies? You have several and you are good at all of them. Or you aren't and you are learning something new. There have to be multiple layers. And they cannot be completely uneven.

If you suck at life, it doesn't matter that you are good at your job. If you suck at your job, you probably cannot afford to be good at life.

I guess I am not so good at the school 'layer' anymore, but when I wrote that, I was doing pretty well. I should add something in there about changing with the times. . .

I scheduled a 3:30 coffee date with my school counselor. It was a coffee date in that I always pick up a coffee on my way in. Maybe 15 years ago my counselor was 6-beers-hot, no-beers average, hence the date part. I had my own plan and I needed to ensure it was foolproof. As long as I got to do things my way, this would be easy or rather more palatable for me.

It was a brisk day so I put on a black jacket with a red plaid scarf. I had red Ray Bans straight out of the 80's and a tootsie pop in my mouth. I had to chew on gum or have something like a pen, a cigarette or a sucker in my mouth. Otherwise, when I stressed out I would bite my fingernails until they bled. I was a nail biter until I came to college and learned that girls don't think torn up fingers are sexy.

The trees on campus were dropping leaves everywhere; the walkways were brown with trampled, dead oak leaves. I don't actually know what kind they were, I made that up, but I think they were oak. Or maple or something.

I had earphones in but my music was off. I figured between the 'music' and the sunglasses I had a bulletproof way to avoid everyone. I was too focused on saving my academic career here at school. If I ruin college, I most likely cannot continue doing what I love, in that I have to keep up a certain level of success, or a good facade. I had good grades, and for about another year I kept up the illusion that I was a decent student, but now I have let it slip. Only a little. No one wants life advice from some asshole who is barely getting by. I could probably manage, but I don't want to get by. I want to win. That is the basis of everything I tell these guys. School is such a great forum and I cannot waste another year and a half of this to hone everything for the real world.

Also, being a student gives me multiple outs: 1) Students live in poverty (for the most part), even some with money, so even though I only make marginally more than the guys who work all the time, I look more successful by leaps and bounds; 2) Since I am in college it is easier to get things from my parents; 3) The university system provides me with a pool of potential clients, and adds thousands to the list every year.

I cannot take any summer classes and next year needs to be as easy as possible so I can prepare for my coming into the world. Between my book and a series of other projects, I cannot afford to spend any spare time wasting my mind on schoolwork. And even though I have shaken off the leash of adolescence, I think my parents would still fucking kill me if I had to pay for a class I already took.

I kept walking, looking as preoccupied as possible, when I saw James in the distance. He was dressed well. A mistake I made very early on in my practice was giving people my fashion advice. It doesn't fit everyone (especially people who pay for fashion advice) and the result was a small army of guys who looked like awkward little clones of me. I got smart and befriended some of the campus fashionistas (see gay) and, to this day, get some input for each individual I was trying to help. They are always happy to make the world classier, they benefit immensely and I have been free to dress like me again.

James' particular style was nerd chic. Most of them turn out kind of that way, but he was better off because of all of the running. He wore form-fitting slacks, sweaters and affordably tailored button up shirts. The only thing he was missing was a pipe.

"Tristan, I cannot thank you enough, man." He reached out to shake my hand. I took the earphones out to acknowledge him. I had to slurp as I said hi because of the tootsie pop.

"It's all you, man. Really. I just helped you get on the right track." I say shit like this all of the time, but I mean it. Sometimes it is so mechanical that I sound like one of those dickheads with plastic hair and a million-dollar smile. But I mean it.

"No man, you really are a god. I mean, you saw what you helped me get."

Pause.

Now you may be thinking that I am a total bastard for what I may do. But I would like to point out that it is not a crime to hang out with a girl. It is also not a crime if she wants to sleep with me just because you may feel sorry for a nerd who got ahead. I am not going to drug her or get her drunk. I am just going to buy her lunch in return for her sharing her expertise with me. If he doesn't fulfill something in her, and she comes to me, it doesn't make me a bad guy.

Play.

"Dude, you know my policy on girls." I tried to sound stern and believable.

"Yeah. No one girl is perfect for anyone our age." He was brilliant. It was verbatim.

My rule about girls is insensitive at times, but perfectly applicable to guys who get heartbroken left and right by very mediocre girls. It is simple: Do not lock yourself into an emotional, monogamous cell when you have no idea what the hell is in her head. She won't love you forever. She won't even love you till graduation, so don't sell yourself short. I tried to put that into the book, but it is too inclusive. I don't want to do this for college students my whole life.

He continued. "I know, man, I know. But for now she is awesome. I would be hard pressed to find a better chick. And when I do, I promise I will upgrade."

Okay, shit. He is a great listener. I have to give it to him. It felt weird to hear someone state my own philosophy so adamantly. For the first time ever, it seemed dangerous.

I didn't like how I felt, so I told him that I was late and had to jet. He said adios and I walked another hundred feet and into the two big doors where all of the counselors had offices. I walked up the narrow stairs. I didn't trust the elevator in this place. On the second level, I walked into the lounge, the off-limits-to-students lounge, and poured myself a 16 oz. Styrofoam cup of Joe. Better than diner coffee but not by much. Enough people over there know me so I could get away with small things like that.

I try often to build bridges. If I were hard pressed to only name my top talents, one of them would definitely be maintaining them.

No one else was around, so I poked my head into her office and she told me to come in and have a seat. It hurts to think about the details of our little talk, even now. But the long and short of it was that I needed an A in poli-sci, I needed to attend all of my classes and I needed to behave. I told her I would try and she stared at me. I told her I would do it with a Rosie the

Riveter fist and she was happy.

 Before I walked out, I turned back to her.

 "What are the odds of getting out of this with less work?"

 "Oh, pretty slim."

 "Are you sure there is no one I can pay off or sleep with?"

 "Goodbye, Tristan."

 "Adios."

 I love this place.

CHAPTER 9

The Economics of It All

Avoid materialistic traps. It is completely unwise to have a bunch of toys and no cash for a date. If you think some girl is going to be impressed by all of your stuff then you are showing her all of the wrong things. A video game system was never a deal breaker in a one-night stand. I am not saying don't do the things you enjoy, but don't put those before a smart buffer of a couple hundred dollars (no date with your new girlfriend should be that expensive).

Another rule of thumb: she pays too. This is not 1954. Women work, have incomes and enjoy dating as well. Don't date girls who make you pay for everything.

I was running late. It was 10:30 and I hadn't done anything to get ready for our 11:00 lunch. Thursday flew by, probably because I actually went to all of my classes, and I did a poli-sci assignment, which physically hurts to say. I also took care of things with Taylor, which made 30 minutes just fly by.

He was a confused guy. If you can imagine that, a student who pays another student for life help does not have his shit together. He was confused but it was mostly just his tunnel vision. For instance, he would not budge when I told him that he shouldn't wear black shoes with a brown belt. It is a very normal thing to know. Even for a heterosexual, anyone who knows something about style knows a rule that has existed since belts and shoes were invented. It was ridiculous that he was so stubborn, but when he finally caved, he suddenly became the fashion police. I try to help losers become cooler, but there is a very painful process at the beginning where I have to deal with them before they become tolerable.

Something I have always hated about what I do is that I occasionally create monsters. I guess that doesn't bother me so much as the fact that I have to deal with those assholes if I want to keep getting paid. Fortunately, they still see me as the master in the grand scheme of things. I almost forgot to call him back after I cut him off the other day, but that was reconciled. He was given a path for the rest of the week.

I came home from poli-sci at about 8:30 and began working on some project. It was more like a weekend homework assignment, but anything bigger than about two pages gets the title 'Project'. It makes it seem like I am doing more work. This new me was a douche. I was doing homework on Friday morning to the point that I almost missed a very hot date. A computer shopping date with a girl who has a boyfriend. Fortunately for me, the phone rang while I was working.

"Hello?"

"Tristan, hey, can I show up 5 minutes late? I have had such a hectic morning." That is when I looked at the clock. Goddamn it.

"Yes, 10 minutes would be better. I have been busy too." I inadvertently used a tip that I give people to do all the time: be "busy" when girls call.

"Okay, great, 11:10. I'll see you soon."

"See you soon."

We hung up and I jumped out of my chair. I had done quite a bit of my schoolwork and showered before class but I had about a 20-minute drive to meet her, so I was still a bit strapped for time.

I already told you my philosophy on how not to be a diva, so I grabbed a black shirt, faded blue jeans and a pair of chuck taylors. I wore a silver watch with a black wristband and

I left my hair slightly disheveled because she seemed like the type. I put on a spritz of—don't judge me—Paris Hilton. I think it is just the right amount of that *je ne sais quoi*. If they don't know what it is, girls always like Paris Hilton. I usually avoid answering the question of what I have on with a guessing game that we never finish. Or I say something like "you can't handle the truth." When I really mean, "you won't sleep with me if you know the truth."

I ran out to my car. It was 10:45. I was pretty sure I would make it, so I did my best not to speed. I sped, but just like normal. Soon enough I was pulling into the parking lot of the computer store. It wasn't too hard to find a spot so I sat for 5 minutes and listened to music until my phone rang.

"I'm watching you." She did her best attempt at a creepy voice.

"Oh, no mister! What do you want with me?" I reciprocated with my best horror movie bimbo.

"I want your liver on a plate with fava beans and a nice Chianti."

"Sorry, I have reserved my liver for a scotch habit I plan on developing in my forties. You can have my lungs instead." I could see her walking over. It was just like the "Birth of Venus," only with clothes on and no giant seashell. We smiled at each other and both hung up. I got out and we hugged. It was natural, like old friends hug. Girls hug me all of the time, but this was different from some freshman who I was going to sleep with before the night was over. It was warmer. Like a real hug. Weird.

"Alright, Ace, what kind of computer are we getting?"

"I have no idea. I just did this so you would come to lunch with me." I laughed after I said it and she laughed too. Many a truth is said in jest.

We walked inside for a pretty simple purchase. I don't know shit about computers (but now I own two), so I did what I could to expedite the shopping and get us out of there. It was nerd hell, but I kept my cool. We ended up talking and joking the whole time, so it wasn't all business. I wasn't there to seduce her, necessarily, so she didn't sense an agenda from me and we just had a good time. She had more personality than the girls I wake up with on Saturday mornings.

We stood there after I paid the $780.00. It was an expensive lunch date, but we had nothing to say for a moment. It was the kind of uncomfortable that isn't so bad, but still in the air.

"So. . .?"

"Yeah," I said. I think that just added to the imaginary tension.

"I'm hungry." She broke the strain, thank God.

"Sandwiches?"

"Sure, I'm up for anything." I looked at her to see if she was up for *anything*, or *anything for lunch*. I think it was a 'moment'. We had a couple so far. Maybe. It's not like I was counting. Was I? Fuck, I don't know. So I ran with it.

"I want to ask you something." I looked serious and my tone was grave.

"Yeah, Tristan?" She sounded serious too, and confused. I leaned in a little bit. Chase leaned in too.

"I, I, uh. . ." I began, "I. . ." I looked at her lips. She looked at mine. She squinted, in thought, and leaned a little more, almost noticeably.

Anticipation.

"I. . .I want to go to that Dago delicatessen on Waterford St." She took a deep breath and agreed with me by nodding. Disappointment is something we all know. It is not always so obvious. But it is. It is easy to sense and I just knew it was there. It was that simple.

"Okay, yeah. Italian place. I know it." She seemed scatterbrained for a second. Another deep breath. We started walking to my car together.

"I can just bring you back to your car when we are done. No use in wasting gas." She nodded again in agreement.

You can dress up. You can work out. You can gel in your hair, wear jewelry and musk, but if you don't know even the most basic psychology you will not go half as far as you are capable.

I opened her car door.

"Sorry, I'm not trying to be chivalrous or anything, my old man just kind of engrained some things in me."

"Why do you do it, Tristan?" I think I knew what she meant. I was taken aback. I stared at her for a second, shut her door and walked around to my side.

"Do what? Listen to my old man still?"

"No, stupid. This. The day planner, the phone calls, the emails," she paused for a second. "James." I was really hoping that his name would not come up today.

"I just do. I can. How many guys my age are improving humanity?"

"Do you know the pressure he puts on himself?" She seemed really concerned. How the hell did she even know?

"He got pretty drunk last night. We went to a party that he said you made him go to. He took me, drank seven beers and was crying by the end of the night. The mood shifted a bit, but I was still in control. I think."

"I tell those guys not to drink." I was pissed he got drunk. I was more pissed that he was an emotional drunk.

"Them? How many of *them* are there?"

"A few. There are a few guys who are actually cool who would love the confidence to meet a girl like you, and I just help them a little."

"Tristan, you are upsetting a very normal balance. Those guys don't need to sleep with 30 girls in college, no one does. But those guys especially don't need to act like little socialites and delude themselves with your 'advice.'"

I laughed. She smiled and punched me in the arm. "What?"

"That is such an easy judgment for a gorgeous blonde to make." I looked over and smiled. "You don't pity nerds because you are a nerd too, just a better looking nerd."

She laughed. "I can see how you get so many girls, T-bag, but that doesn't work on me." She was blushing.

"T-bag?"
"Yeah, your new name."

CHAPTER 10

Tristan,

You don't know me, but I am in your film class. That's probably why you don't know me. My buddy told me about some 'extracurricular' activities you sponsor and I was wondering if there I was any way I could get on bored. I don't want to waste your time now with all of the details, but I would be glad to talk with you in person.

Jesse

He wrote 'on bored'. I didn't know whether to laugh at him or cry for the $75,000 he already owes the university system that has clearly not done him too much good. I was always willing to take on a new challenge, but I really didn't know if I was going to have the time to carry so many clients *and* focus on school. The timing was horrible. I needed to sit on it for a while. He has waited this long, what's another week?

I sat waiting in a small common area for students that was near the campus bookstore. They sold coffee, average deli food and decent personal pizzas. It was nothing like Angie's, but good enough for those times when lethargy or finances prevented the 10-minute walk to quality. It was a brisk day and I was still chilled from the walk over, so I warmed my hands with a small black coffee while I thought about Alex's problem.

He was attractive to women, he had a job (money), he

had good enough style and was witty. He essentially had everything that I offer up when guys need my help, except the money thing. He had, instead, a mild stutter. It was a confidence-crushing problem that a speech therapist could easily save him from. If he went to a speech therapist, however, he would not give me money to help him, so I was going to give it a shot. I mean, I was not stopping him from getting professional help. Who knows? Maybe he already has one. I'm sure his parents sent him to one at some point. He needed something else that professionals can't offer: confidence with girls.

I don't have a format and I don't use a specific structure for helping these guys. I do use certain words that make this more palatable, more doable for them; I say 'ideas' and 'concepts', so that at the end of the day it sounds like we just had a brainstorming session for life and they are not paying me for 'life coaching.' It was a pretty simple concept, but it worked. To them it just feels like I am giving them ideas to succeed in areas of life that they normally suck at.

Alex walked in and sat down with me. He looked a bit tired.

He knew that I knew because he started with "Yeah, I I I was up la la late."

"Why?"

"Sssschool."

"Alright, let's get down to business. Coffee?" He nodded. "This one's on me." Tokens of friendship made this what it is. "Al, you have the right look, you are funny, you only need to make one change."

"Le le let me gue guess what tha that is." When he laughed a little, I knew instantly that my plan was sure fire because a cute blonde sitting close to us (a spot I strategically chose) looked at him and grinned. She was alone doing homework—Child Psychology. These girls were everywhere on our campus. They were cute, bleeding hearts, who liked sweet guys. I failed miserably with them for a long time until I figured out that they weren't the drunk liberal arts girls I was normally successful with. They don't like arrogant cool-guys. They like nice guys, project guys. Alex was both. I was more of the latter and when I learned how to show it I did very well for myself.

Over the years, I learned to quit looking at the girl and to start noticing her surroundings, clothes, friends, textbooks. A girl sitting alone with a book can tell you more from 10 feet away without speaking than a girl who you just spent an hour trying to get through to.

I talked to Alex about my idea while we got up and got a coffee. I told him the psychology behind my plan to expose him to more of those girls, all of them, and he could go from there. Don't change you. Change the scenery. A city boy can't get many country girls, so he needs to find them in a city. He liked the idea, so we needed to figure out where to find them. On our way back to the table, coffee in hand, I kept walking and sat with the cute Child Psychology girl. He sat too. He lost the flare. His enthusiasm for my idea was consumed by his fear of talking to new girls. We all get that. I just hide it well.

"Can I ask you a few questions?"

She was as taken back as Al, but we were going to fight through this. I would be the linchpin of calm and these two kids could fall madly in love in the meantime. Or at least want to bang.

"Hum, sure. What about?"

"What kind of clubs are you in?" I have this very specific look that I give when I ask these kinds of questions. I squint, barely, and inflect in such a way that it sounds like I am talking to an old friend rather than some new girl. It is an amazing tool into the female psyche.

"Well, I am in the religious studies club, and I volunteer at the elementary schools here." She was getting more comfortable. There is nothing closer to a girl's element than herself. Keep her in her element. She looked at him when she spoke. They needed some commonality. . .

I looked at Al and said "Hey, weren't you going to do something like that?" He looked at me confused. He was an atheist. But after about three seconds, he was an atheist who saw where I was going with it. And before he could stutter an answer I cut him off; "It is so hard to find extracurricular when you don't know the right people."

"There are posters for clubs everywhere." She looked at me like I was bullshitting a little too much.

"Anyone can read a poster," I looked at her name on the top of a piece of paper, "but, Candice, if you just go by posters, all of the clubs are the best and that's just not true." The name was a good touch. I do that often.

She smiled. He looked at me, amazed. I was striking up a conversation, and to most of my clients, it was magic.

I kept the magic up. "So, what other clubs are you in?" I paused for a moment, then added, "You know, we should leave you alone, you are studying and we are just bothering."

"You're fine." She liked the attention. We all would. Otherwise, we would not study in public; we would do it at home. "I wanted to do the exchange program and study in France."

He took a cue. "So, ssso you sp speak French?"

"A little. I am in French 4. I actually think my French is pretty horrible."

"I I I'm sure it's it's b better tha than my E English." And he laughed. She smiled. Own it Alex. Be you.

"Awe, don't say that. I hardly even noticed." She liked it. Inasmuch as a person can like a handicap, an impediment, an evolutionary speed bump.

And on that note I excused myself. I had to give him a chance to shine or crash, but it would be better either way if I was not there for it. I ceded him the field. That was good enough for today. I said goodbye to our new friend and said adios to Al.

When I made my exit, I got a text from Stevo. He was a friend in my sense of the word. He was manipulative, good with girls and an absolutely psycho drunk. I quit drinking with him after waking up in the back of a car he 'borrowed' and parked four miles out of town. He played kidnapper with me when I passed out at a party. He then walked back into town and passed out in the quad at 7am. Campus security woke him up at 7:30. His daddy was well known, so nothing happened. That is a recurring theme with kids of his background. My parents were more normal, so I had to get out of shit on my own.

MARGARITAS, PAJAMAS, MAYBE COKE. CALL ME. STVO

He knew I didn't do that either, but it did tell me that a lot of party girls were going to be there. I wanted to go, but I didn't. I had work to do so that I could pass the 15th grade. Also, the first thing that I thought of was Chase. I know that sounds lame. I guess it was, but I did.

I looked at my watch. I mean, I did get a lot done this morning. Maybe I could just go and say hi. No matter how I looked at it, I had a reputation to keep up. If I didn't go, it would be bad for my clients to find out that I did homework on a weekend instead of being me.

Maybe I will just drop by and say hi. Make an appearance, so to speak.

CHAPTER 11

Every guy thinks he is good in bed. Fall into this trap. Yes, you heard me right: Think that with every grain of your being. If you are not, don't worry. If you think you are, it shows in your walk, and your talk and your laugh and in the way you address others. Girls can smell this out and after misleading enough ladies about how good you actually are you may learn something along the way. Practice makes perfect. You aren't going to get any practice by being honest and upfront about sleeping with one heavy girl your senior year of high school just so you wouldn't come to college a virgin. Don't worry about mentioning that your first run is never more than a minute. It won't be, eventually. Don't worry about much at all. Worry is ugly. Girls sleep with us for fun. I think there are some other reasons too, but for simplicity's sake, think about the fun aspect for now.

I woke up with cottonmouth. It was bad. I always brush my teeth before I go to bed, and I could tell by the taste in my mouth that I hadn't. It wasn't really hangover because I never had more than a few drinks, but I had this thing about brushing my teeth. I feel disgusting if I don't. The problem was I was not in my room. I didn't have a toothbrush here.

I was lying next to Laura, the brunette at the coffee shop from earlier this week. She did end up going with me to the party. I think what happened is her plan fell through, and she called me as a backup. We had fun. I related to her. I was understanding and curious. I timed everything well. I introduced her to a lot of people and looked like a social god for the evening. And then I kept her up for about three hours after we left the party. I was not too torn up about being her plan B, well, mostly because I kept her up for three hours after the party.

I got out of her bed completely naked and walked to her bathroom. She had an apartment on the edge of campus. I could see the school chapel from her window. I hoped someone there would see me standing there naked. I got myself a large drink of cold water and grabbed her toothbrush. Rather, one of the two that was in there.

"Tristan?" she called from her room. "My roommate is home."

That meant put on a towel. Or it meant leave so her roommate doesn't know she slept with a boy last night. I was pretty sure the whole building knew what we did last night. Either way, I put on the pink robe that was hanging on the bathroom door.

I was brushing my teeth and walked into her room.

"Are you using my toothbrush?" First off, good guess me.

"Do you remember where I put my tongue last night? You still kissed me. This is just a toothbrush." I said this with toothpaste still in my mouth and my head tilted slightly back to keep it in. "Oh, yeah. Thank you by the way."

I smiled. She was number 100. Yes, I count. I wondered if I should tell her the honors. Probably not. To my credit, I was always safe and responsible. As safe and responsible as a guy can be after sleeping with 100 girls. I subtracted three huge mistakes from the statistic. Huge being the operative word.

"How many condoms did we use?" I looked at the floor. It was peppered with wrappers. I hoped instantly that they were all mine.

And then came the words I have heard 80 out of 100 times: "I don't normally do that."

Yeah, I know, honey. You and the rest of this campus. "I had a lot of fun, Laura. You are pretty cool when you want to be." I grinned and she threw a pillow at me. We laughed and spent about another hour just being lazy and talking. I spent about half of the time wishing that she was Chase. Oh well. Soon enough. I try casually to point out that we are not dating but I do so without the uncomfortable, patronizing 'talk' about what happened. That is so high school. I think I was as good at this talk as I was in bed.

As I put my clothes back on and gave her a kiss goodbye I told her that we should keep in touch, and if she ever wanted to grab a coffee to call me.

"Tristan?"

What the hell was it? If there was a time when a girl went psycho in this game, it was when we first woke up, which we skated through with flying colors, and at my exit, when 10 different pieces of reality sank in at the same time.

"Can you put my roommate's robe back in the bathroom? She will be pretty pissed off if she knew my one night stand was in it."

Classic.

I took a shower when I got back to my place. I had a coffee date with James. And given my four hours of spooning in a single bed with almost no pillow, coffee was the order of the day. He seemed to be doing well, so I didn't think I was going to be able to help him too much anymore. I can usually sense it after a few months. I never have a client longer than about four months or the second girl he sleeps with, whichever comes first. In James' case, it was about three weeks to the four-month point.

While I was shaving, my phone rang. Dustin.

"Hey."

"Hey, T."

"What can I do for you, man?"

"I don't think anyone can do much, man. I just wanted to know what you would do if you found out your old man was cheating on your mom." He sounded deep into the bottle.

"Oh shit, Dustin, I'm sorry. When did you find out?"

"Yesterday. I have been drunk since then. I guess I don't give a fuck, but why the fuck would someone do that?" He sounded really messed up.

I am pretty sure the whore who broke his heart cheated on him too. I say 'pretty sure' because I don't listen when he talks about her. As I said, I am not his therapist. I am his friend for hire.

"I don't know, man. Are you okay? What do you want me to say?" It was a compulsory statement that usually came out during the feelings portion of any talk. I didn't mean for it to come out this time.

"Fuck, man, I don't know. I am just fucking, I don't know." I think I heard a few sobs.

He hung up. I wasn't going to play games so I made a note to myself to call him back later and hopefully he would be sober. Soberer.

My parents were still together. I had no idea what divorce was like or the cheating or the broken households or any of that. I think my parents still went on dates even. I had no idea what to tell Dustin but there were plenty of people I could ask. Say about 60 percent of the American population. Better yet, he could ask them because it was his problem. I don't know how to deal with that kind of stuff.

I *did* know that I had about 20 minutes to meet James and I had a five-minute walk in the cold autumn air. I finished shaving and then I did my best to completely dry my hair, but it was never enough. It was always that much colder when I first walked outside. In a few weeks, it would not be cold anymore; it would be fucking frost in my hair. I refuse to blow dry it too. The shoe thing might *come off* as effete or gay, but the blow-drying of one's hair is almost entirely gay. Not an issue here at our progressive campus, but not my alley. Especially not to the detriment of my number one and two past times: sleeping with girls and getting paid to tell others how to sleep with girls.

I walked to where James was going to meet me. I wanted to fend off the cold that was going to catch me soon enough with the mildly colder change in weather, so I ordered a tea. The tea came quickly, and James walked in. He pat me on the back and asked how my computer was. It took me a second to register. Oh, yeah, Chase. It was still in the box.

"It's great, man. You know how to pick them."

"Computers or girls?" He laughed at his own joke. It was funny enough, I guess.

"What's on the agenda today?"

"Well, the colder it gets, the less I run, which is fine. It's more time with Chase."

"What about your game, man? Don't forget that small detail."

"Yeah, it's fine, but if you had to pick, obviously, you would pick the girl too, right?"

"Yeah, of course." Of course I would rather be drawn and quartered in a medieval town square than design a video game. . ."But I don't put all of my stock in one girl. Ever."

"I know. I guess I shouldn't be such a chump." He thought about it for a second. "But God! Look at her." He looked off, imagining her. I wanted to slap him.

"Well, man, your goals are not to get married and have two kids by the end of next year. They were to run a marathon, bang a few pretty girls and design that game. I don't say this because I don't want you to see her." That was a lie. "I'm saying it because if, God forbid, it doesn't work out, which is a statistical fact, then you are back at square one. No video game, and out of shape because you stopped everything for her." How many fucking times am I going to give this talk to these guys?

I think the answer is: The rest of my life.

He acted like he saw the light, and for once I was happier to talk about video games and other nerdy bullshit than about girls. Mainly because I wanted to sleep with the girl that he was betting everything on.

I say he acted because he dropped her name seventeen more times. It was irritating, but I didn't show irritation. I guess it pissed me off because I was not only trying to sleep with Chase; it was that I really thought she and I could have had a relationship. She was awesome. And it was a waste of her awe-

someness to date a clingy nerd. He was going to stalk her when they broke up and it would be awful for everyone. The other side of that coin is that he was seriously talented with computers. And while that is a meaningless skill to me, it is something he needs to pursue. Every fucking moron our age was chasing ass, but he could do both. He was one of the few who could get a girl (just not Chase).

Chapter 12

Self-image

This important aspect of being a modern guy is a double-edged sword. Do not be consumed by it. It should never dictate what you do. This should supplement it. Self-image should always be something you are aware of, but never focus on.

When people try to create a self-image they go overboard and turn a good style point into a lifestyle. They turn a fashion statement into an enormous amount of pressure to act a certain way. Don't act. Be.

I ate a power bar after my tea. I thought I wanted coffee, but tea hit the spot. I figured an hour in the gym would give me a little pick-me-up. I wasn't as tired as just feeling lazy. I always did, after waking up in a strange bed. It was my equivalent of a hangover. I would go to the gym, work on some of my academics and call Chase. I wanted to talk to her for the last few days, but it never happened. I was actually hoping that she would call me. Something I would never say out loud.

As I was changing into my gym clothes, a wave of tired came over me. I yawned. I knew that the second I sat down I was going to nap the entire afternoon away. I don't do that. I do, but as the great exception, not a rule. And never more than once every couple of weeks. Instead of being a lifestyle for me, it is a small reward to be lazy for an afternoon. I should have had the goddamn coffee.

I decided to try my hand at a shake. People have those all of the time before they go to the gym. I began to rummage through my stuff. I never kept copious amounts of food around, but I figured a few pieces of fruit would do the trick. Hum. . .Okay, do they put oatmeal in shakes? I think so. It has fiber or something in it. I emptied a pack of Maple Syrup and Brown Sugar Oatmeal in a banana, 4 strawberries (I threw the rest away), and a cup of milk.

Voilà! It was mediocre and I don't think it gave me any energy. I did give it a college try, and I achieved my subconscious goal of putting the gym off for another twenty minutes. I also felt full of power bar and milkshake. There was no way I was going to make it if I kept thinking about it.

Out the door, off like a shot. It was a 10-minute walk across campus to get there. A significantly better gym was a short drive away, but the corporate gyms have dedicated athletes. The campus gym had freshmen girls who wanted people to look at them. I was glad to oblige, and I usually left there with a new friend, a new number or a sore chest, arms and back. I wasn't ever crazy about fitness, but I keep myself in check. I work out maybe twice a week. I owe it to the girls I bed down with to at least keep up some level of fitness.

When I got there, it was a sausage fest. There were about seven guys in the small little workout room. I immediately regretted my decision to show up in that these guys were going to cuss at each other, size each other up the whole time and act like animals about pressing out one more rep. I wonder if nerds ever do the same thing with their programs or whatever lame shit they do—'You type that algorithm! What? What, you little faggot? You can't do it? Too hard? Gimme one more line of code! C'mon. C'mon, that's right. Do this one for you! Do it for me!'

I was amused with myself, but that didn't change the fact that there were too many 'tards eye-fucking each other in those tight Under Armour shirts. I walked into the little room off to the side with the elliptical.

Hello, pretty blonde girl! And thank you, Lord. It's taboo

to hit on girls who are working out. It's unspoken, but known. However, there are certain outfits that when coupled with a very slow pace on a machine, which is already not a real workout, that just screams "talk to me, Tristan." I could see her timer was at 38 minutes and she hadn't broken a sweat. I know why she was here, even without her constantly looking at me. She was probably waiting for one of the guys in the other room to talk to her before I got here, but I don't think she realizes that they were interested in something else.

I jumped on the elliptical next to her. "I wish it were nicer out," I said. "I would much prefer to run." We all know I don't run. I do pass for someone who runs 10 miles a week though. I am told I look like I play sports. I think sex and walking everywhere are my only real workouts.

"I know, right?" She seemed dumb. Not to pass judgment on girls who work out, just this one.

"I was actually hoping these would be full so I had an excuse to go back to my apartment and read by the fire. I love to do that when it's muggy out."

"You have a fireplace in your apartment?"

"No, I usually just build a small one in a trash can in my living room. It has the same effect."

I didn't like her laugh. I think I was just in a bad mood. I always thought I handled pressure well, but the school thing has been in the back of my mind constantly. Even last night, when I was throwing Laura around in her bed, my situation occurred to me a couple of times. That's not normal.

I think I should call Chase. What was she going to do for me? I don't know, I guess I just wanted to call. It didn't matter. I don't know what I thought. I was just confused. I felt like I was being pulled 20 different ways and I didn't know which five to choose.

My heart rate was 104 according to the digital readout. I looked at the girl next to me. "Take it easy." I jumped off the elliptical after racking up a staggering 1.7 kilometers. I had to get out of there. She looked at me a little confused.

I walked out and passed all of the jocks. I went outside and sat on a bench. I needed a plan. I needed to go back to my room and. . .Fuck it. I just wanted a nap. But it wasn't going to happen quite yet.

I reached into my pocket and grabbed my cell phone. I did it. I was tired of waiting and I had to do it. I called Chase. The phone rang 6 times, which felt like an excessive amount to me, and then went to her voicemail. I didn't know what to say. I wasn't expecting an answering machine on a Saturday afternoon. But then again, I guess nerds have to supply internet 24-7. I just told her it was me and to call back when she could.

I hung up and immediately my phone rang.

"Sorry, I was in the shower. I just went for a run. What's up? How's the computer?" I pictured her standing there in a towel.

"Uh, it's fine. I was actually just leaving the gym myself." It didn't seem necessary to tell her about my 1.7 K on the elliptical.

"I'll bet you are one of those pretty boys who watches the mirror while working out and fantasizes about himself. Is that it?"

"You had me pegged. I thought we knew each other, but we must really know each other." We both laughed and went quiet.

"When are you taking me out again?" I didn't know if I heard right. Holy shit. I think I did, but, really?

"Gosh, I guess soon. I hope you aren't planning anything immoral. I am saving myself for marriage." I say that about once a week. It is always funny and always sounds like a challenge.

"Lunch again?"

"Yeah, I think daylight is safest when I am with you. My friends might start to think things if I am seen with you at night."

"You? Your friends? Do you know how many people have told me to avoid you, Tristan?"

"Obviously not enough." I was slick. I do well for myself, but this was amazing. I think I liked this girl. I just didn't know how to go about this. "When is good for you?"

"You are the busy one, Mr. Lifecoach. When can you pencil me in? I think Tuesday is good for me. How does that sound?"

"Hmmm. I guess I can move some people around and give you Tuesday at lunch."

"Well then, it's lunch on Tuesday."

"See you then."

"Bye."

Was it really this easy? My life has been pretty easy. Well, barring the horrific academic situation I got myself into, but even with a little care and love that hasn't been so bad. I just need to shuffle my priorities. No, I just need to shift my focus a bit. I still have a small enterprise to run. I cannot lose sight of all of the people who need me. Their lives would probably come crashing down if I were to quit on them.

I would find out later that I have the opposite effect sometimes.

CHAPTER 13

Jesse,

Hey, it's Tristan. I got your email and I am glad you are thinking about making some changes. I don't know exactly how busy my schedule is going to be with the end of the quarter coming up, but I would like get some information from you and see what we are dealing with.

It's not necessarily an easy process, and I don't know if anyone told you about pricing, but that is something you need to consider before we go any further with this.

If you think you are ready, and can finance this journey, I would be glad to take a look at what we need to do to improve your situation, and we could go from there.

Tristan

I never thought I had a negative impact on anyone's life. I was always someone that people thanked for being the way I am. I just had sex with a girl I met a few days ago and the first words out of her mouth were "thank you". I guess it is all of the giving without being self-aggrandizing. I didn't need to brag to her before the deed. She would eventually find out. I didn't brag to nerds that I was cool. I just told them I could help them.

I assume, since it is usually the top 5% of our class that usually employ my services, that they are smart enough to fill in the blanks when I leave something unsaid. I equate things like condoms to seatbelts and assume that intelligent adults wear them. *Another phone call.*

"Tristan? Hey, it's Rob."

"Hey man. How are you? How are things?"

"Things are: I'm joining the fucking marines because of you."

"I don't remember ever suggesting that." I was taken aback, but I have had this 'fuck you, Tristan' talk once or twice. I knew how to keep my cool.

"Do you remember a girl named Jessica, maybe you introduced us? Maybe she was looking to get fucking pregnant from the first guy with a job that came along, and you knew it when you told her about me."

In a last ditch effort not to look like I did him no good, I introduced him to some very loose girls from a vocational school about 45 minutes away. You're probably asking why I don't normally just do that to give these guys an esteem boost. It would be easier for me. Well, I don't. It's not my M.O. They pay me pretty well for help. It's not always about girls either. Some of these guys want to fit in. They want to be like me. They want to feel accepted and we do it the natural way. Well, as natural as I can make it. For him, it was about the girls. And apparently he got one.

"Look, if you won't own it, fine. Blame me. Blame me because you don't know the first thing about fucking safe sex and you wouldn't know what the fuck to do without someone holding your hand. Do I need to show you how to do it? Should I hold your hand next time you screw some townie?!" I almost never lost my shit like that, but I felt defensive. I was breathing hard. My heart rate actually went up. Who needs the elliptical?

"She won't get rid of it. I can't afford this and school. What the fuck was I supposed to do?" I could hear him start to cry. I think it was seasonal. Dustin cried too. I need to call him.

"I'm sorry, man. I can't change that. What do you want me to say?"

"Fuck you, Tristan. Fuck you."

After he hung up, I thought about what he was actually going through. I really thought I had school problems. He is shit out of luck, though.

Did I really do that to him? He should have known. Right? What was I supposed to say? 'Watch out, this chick is going to lock you down.' I knew they were known for that in said small town, but I didn't know *she* was. He chose to join the Marines. How was I the bad guy here?

It messed me up. I remembered again that I needed to call Dustin, but I was already in a shitty mood. I wasn't his crutch. Next thing I knew, he was going to blame me for his parents split.

I found as I got older that Type A personalities are always the scapegoats. I got blamed for things I was never involved in because I was an easy target. Teachers blame me for rowdy classes because I'm a smart ass and must have instigated things. My parents held me accountable for my little sister's behavior because it was easier to yell at me than to deal with her melt-downs. I just let things roll off, but if they don't roll fast enough, they built up and that's what I felt like now.

I tried to sit and bury myself in required reading. That lasted all of two minutes.

Dustin was too smart for his own good, anyways. That was why he had trouble fitting in. People like him had a core group of friends in high school and those friends accepted that he was a dickhead who had to be right all of the time and that he would always correct them. They didn't fit in either, so it was a mutually beneficial relationship. I guess, in kind of a sad, nerdy way.

He didn't have those guys as a freshman here and needed some help. I gave it to him. I made about $700 from him in just over a month of trying to help him. I sort of gave up on him towards the end because he thought he knew more than I did about what I was trying to tell him and wanted to contend every single piece of information I shared with him.

I drifted off that night. Everything was weird. I was happy about Chase, but I couldn't think of anything but Robbie. He could have made any one of those mistakes without me around. People do it all the time. Why is it my fault? It wasn't my fault. I just couldn't say it enough to believe it.

CHAPTER 14

Cheap lessons

Don't buy into the moral crossroads. People want you to believe that you are responsible for everything that happens. It is always those people who want to control everything. When those same people acknowledge that they don't control everything they believe that God controls everything else, and that they can influence him—more control. Let go of this illusion as soon as you can.

You are responsible for what YOU do. Don't forget that part. I cannot explain why adults don't act like adults. There is nothing noble about taking on some contrived burden for your fellow man's (or especially woman's) actions. If the girl you are about to sleep with isn't adult enough to take half of the credit, then you shouldn't be with her. Period.

I am pretty sure that is the only ethical standpoint I have. And as much as I believe it, what Robbie said really hit me hard. I guess not so much what he said, but what he was doing. I wanted a way to forget it and over the next couple of days I managed to get it out of my mind here and there, but never completely.

Things felt slow. I couldn't explain it. The weather was deteriorating into muggy cold. Rushing season was in full swing, which didn't affect me much, but was still annoying. It felt like a labor to do what I do. I didn't have the energy to focus on school, chase Chase, do my work, and make cameos at a respectable amount of social gatherings. I was running out of steam, but

I was lunching with Chase today and I was hopeful that it would recharge my batteries.

We met at her job. She was wearing a white polo shirt with a nametag. I was glad to point out that she looked like a bigger nerd than ever.

"I hope to God you have a jacket," I said.

"Is it still cold? It wasn't so bad this morning."

"No, it's just that you look a little too much like a computer programmer." She punched me in the arm and we walked outside and got into my car.

"Take me back to my apartment if you could. I want to get something there."

"A new shirt?" I was on a roll.

"Something like that. Maybe a new friend for lunch? I may have one of those lying around." I really liked her grin. I egged her on for the pleasure of seeing that smile. I was on the verge of becoming very lame.

It was a short trip to her place—a modest apartment, but her own. Most people our age had roommates. She was tidy, but the place looked like a pretty typical girl's pad. She didn't own a TV. I didn't see a computer either. I was trying to figure her out and was transfixed by what she did and didn't have when she interrupted me.

"You did want me to get rid of this, right?" She took off her shirt and led me to her room.

I kissed her. "Yes. I. Did." More kissing. Then her jeans, mine, my shirt and then her bra. Her bra was guilty of hiding two of the most perfectly formed breasts God ever put on a woman. She didn't mince words and didn't play shy. I was still in a state of shock when I was thrown down on her bed and told what to do. She treated me like a toy and showed no concern for my well-being, stamina or safety. Stamina was foremost.

She knew what she wanted. She was not shy. She had no reason to be. Chase asked, told, pulled and pushed me around to get exactly what she needed. I was happy to help, but it was like dancing with someone who wanted to lead. I usually lead, so this was uncharted territory. Wonderful, loud, biting, scratching uncharted territory. Time stopped. It was almost surreal. I don't think I gave her the three-hour performance that I pulled off the other night. I was actually lucky to give her 10 minutes. Unless she was a great actress, I know she got what she wanted. . .3 times.

The natural progression ended with us lying side by side under the covers. We were breathing hard and she looked like she was thinking. I didn't want to ask because there were too many things I did not want to potentially talk about. After about a minute, she got up, walked naked to the window and opened it a few inches. The cold breeze felt great and did wonders for cooling the place off. I pulled the sheets back so she could get back in, then I rolled on my side to get closer to her.

She lay back down and looked at me: "Where are you taking me for lunch, Stud?"

"Oh, yeah, about that. . .I have this hot date soon, so I need to cut lunch short."

"Oh, do I know her?" Insert 'your mom' here.

"Yeah, she's the Dean. I need to graduate soon enough and things aren't looking so bright. I need an assist." I was smoking hot in bed and funny. I know why people love me. I really do.

"I can make sandwiches here. We don't have to leave. I just need to be back at work by 2."

"I'll see what I can do."

I went home after I dropped her off at work. We cut it kind of close because I couldn't stop kissing her after we got back into bed. The sex was great. Lunch was good and the dessert sex was even better. I was in the best mood I had been in for years. Sometimes, even when something shitty was going on there was still this silver lining in the clouds. Or, there were just a few clouds in a silver sky. I don't know if that analogy works, but I think most people would get the point.

I walked into my room. It looked different. Brighter. I hadn't thought about fucking Robbie's life up all day, and I was almost motivated to be successful in a way that would impress Chase (read: school). I sat down at my desk, took a deep breath and tried to make myself want to actually work on a paper about Peru. I turned my computer on. After this bullshit assignment, I was going to copy-edit some of my book for submission to another publisher who seemed more receptive. In that I mean they didn't blatantly reject me when I emailed them.

I brought up my email and instantly my world got smaller. Everything changed in a few seconds. I don't know where to start. I got the most fucked up email I have ever gotten in my adult life. Not one of those Donkey Show videos or one of those really dirty spams that come up occasionally.

I used to help a guy named Ashleigh. Ash. He was another one of those guys that didn't know how to translate his intellect into a social life. I was still kind of new at this, so I gave him some contrary advice. I thought if he just changed who he was a little and acted a different way he would be fine. It didn't really work for getting him laid, but he made more friends and he eventually found his niche.

Those friends were the group of guys that I thought would expose him to the kinds of girls that he would not have a hard time sleeping with. They were a receptive group of dudes who liked fresh blood and even benefited from him because cokeheads occasionally need help with their schoolwork. He found some decent girls. He made new friends and after he started doing coke I quit helping him. It was my other backup when guys were impossible. I thought cokeheads would kill a know-it-all like Robbie, so he got what he got, but Ash would turn out fine.

People knew that I introduced him to those guys. It wasn't a controversial fact, but it was known. I was buddies with a few of them through Stevo, and had no problem introducing Ash at a low- key house party. It was fine. I didn't force the coke into his nose, I didn't tell him to do it. I even said once that I don't do it because of all of the shit that can go wrong. So he knew the dangers.

He was fine for a while. He was just another dude. Plenty of those guys do hard drugs, get out of college and grow up. They go on to be successful and someone as smart as him should have had no problem with that formula.

He fucking died last night.

His mom emailed me. I don't know how she got my email address. I don't know how she knew to blame me for his social ties. That was over a year ago. I don't know anything about him or his death except that he OD'ed last night, and that I am apparently the culprit.

I didn't feel responsible at first. But God damn it. His mother BLAMED me. She said that he never would have done something like that until he met me. I felt tears welling up. She said that I pulled him away from school and his bright future to snort drugs and sleep with teenagers. I did do that. I started to feel worse and worse.

I did that stuff. Everything she said was true. I didn't kill him, but I was just as much to blame as his drug dealer, whom he met through me. I didn't introduce him so he could deal the shit to Ash. I did it so he could have some friends that were a little more crazy and fun. Fuck. I felt sick. I was sick.

I threw up in the trashcan next to my computer desk. I started to cry. Not for him, I guess, but for everything. For his mom and his family. They were probably doing the same thing right now. She probably dropped him off at school thinking about how well he would do, and how he was inevitably going to graduate with honors and make everyone proud. Now he's at the coroner's, tricked out with blow. Not so smart after all, huh, Ash?

I was still wrenching, but it wasn't enough. I could hardly breathe. What the fuck good have I done? What have I done? Was Taylor going to end up like this? What about James? He believes in me. Was I going to kill him next? There were shit loads of people out there with baggage that I created. I don't know how this happened. Ash was a nerd who wanted more friends. That's all.

I needed to see Chase again. I figured she would understand.

CHAPTER 15

Approach

Your approach to everything should be consistent. That is something everybody appreciates: consistency. I don't mean everything has to be the same and that you cannot be fun and spontaneous. You should be. But there are 16 different personalities according to some psychologists and there are a 100 according to others. If you fall into one or a couple, then do not, DO NOT try to come off as something completely different. You can get away with a lot if you are always consistent.

If you dress up or change the way you do things when you meet someone, they will wonder what happened to you when you go back to being normal you. If you use some extra outgoing, made-up personality to get a girl, she is not going to sleep with you after you revert back to you. The best approach is to be outgoing, but not an extravagant lie. Girls don't sleep with caricatures, not more than once.

I slept in. I missed a class this morning. I sent an email with the assignment to the professor. I didn't care if he cared or not. I felt like shit. My stomach hurt from throwing up last night and I was thirsty. I had no water bottles in my fridge and I didn't normally drink tap water. I saw beer and orange juice. I opted for tap water.

It was time for me to get away. I was contemplating leaving school. I wanted to get out of that place and not check my email and not talk to anyone. I didn't want Stevo to come by and give me my weekly invite to something ridiculous. I didn't want Taylor calling me for advice at 1 am while he was standing outside at a party about to make a move. Which is something he has done about twice a month since I met him.

I grabbed my car keys to leave. As I walked to the door, I tried to think of where I was going to go. I didn't know. I put them down and sat at my desk.

I couldn't get a hold of Chase the night before. I left her a message and I sounded really screwed up. I didn't know why she wouldn't call me back. She had to have been home that night. What the hell could she have been doing? I never asked questions about girls like that. There was always another one to turn to, but I didn't want to do that this time. I wanted *her*.

As my problems became more real and more fucked up and as the severity of every revelation increased, I wanted stable ground. I didn't want it. I needed it. I stayed up at night thinking of Ash. I thought about how I ruined his life and how I completely ruined Robbie's life and I thought about how I was probably ruining Taylor, James and Dustin's lives. I think James already had a reason to kill me, and if my understanding of the progression was correct, I was going to be the next to die.

School. Robbie. Ashleigh. James kills me. I didn't feel bad for James. I had it too deeply ingrained in me that Chase was mine the moment she wanted me more than him. I did feel a pang of conscience that he trusted me and I backdoored him, but if he learned anything from me he could rebound in a day. I had faith in him. Hopefully that would be enough.

Chase finally called:

"Hey, are you okay? I was at a girlfriend's last night and didn't hear my phone. I saw your call this morning. You sounded bad. Did I scare you?" She laughed a little. I didn't feel like laughing but I tried.

"No, a buddy OD'ed. I didn't know what to do. I guess I just wanted to talk."

"You can talk to me now, Tristan." The problem was I had

nothing to say. Was I going to tell her that he OD'ed because of me? 'Hey, I technically killed someone; I hope this doesn't affect our relationship'. Not the topic I wanted to stay on.

"No, I'm okay now I guess. I just felt really shitty last night." I had to change the subject. I still felt knots in my stomach thinking about the email. "How was your friends'? Did you talk about me?"

"As a matter of fact I did."

"Anything good?"

"Yeah, she helped me with a pregnancy test."

"Oh yeah? Do you have one of those bodies that know within a few hours that you are pregnant? I thought it took like a month or something."

"Yeah, an angel told me, and now you have to give up being Mr. Cool and raise our child while I program computers for a living."

"I don't think you want me influencing anyone's life, Chase." My stomach sank as I said it.

"Oh, I know I don't. I will leave you specific instructions each day." Her humor was always on point, but what killed me was that when she implied that we would have a monogamous relationship I didn't cringe. "Really, is everything okay?"

"Yeah, these things work themselves out." I couldn't talk about it yet. Or ever.

"Well, whatever it is I recommend that you bury yourself in schoolwork and ride it out. You aren't going to do yourself any good taking your own advice. Unless your problem is that you can't meet chicks." Dig.

"I meet okay chicks. Average ones. Nerds even, but I meet them." I didn't feel funny, but I promise myself every day that I will not forget how great I am.

"Call me anytime, Tristan. I mean it."

"Yeah, I will. When can I see you again?"

"Whenever you want."

"I'll call soon."

We hung up and I sat there. I think I was in a relationship with her. I didn't know. I wondered if she had broken up with James. I wanted to ask her, but I didn't say his name when we were together. I could ask him, but I don't think he would appreciate it. I would wait. I had a few days before he and I were supposed to meet. I would bring it up later.

She was right. I should just buckle down, pass school and figure something out along the way. It's not like I was going to save Ash now by crying myself to sleep every night. I sure as hell was not going to fix Robbie's issue but I was sweating it. I guess I let them put their problems on my shoulders and it was okay as long as they paid me. I wasn't mature enough to help them. None of us knew what we were doing. I was just better at hiding it.

For once, I was going to take someone else's advice and buckle down. School wasn't hard. I just hated the amount of time it would take to do the dumbest shit. I didn't learn anything relevant when I read what they wanted me to. It almost never applied to something that I was supposed to be studying. But for some reason, this snob professor wanted me to spend my weekend buried under three books—books I was required to buy because he was friends with the authors.

I was going to crawl out of my own skin. I decided that I would not attend any parties for a week or two. I would also not take on any new work for a while. I would keep trying to publish my book. Someone would see the light eventually. I suppose it is best to keep my 'victims' out of the limelight for now.

About the Author
Tristan was a mildly successful student who single-handedly got 80 nerds laid while sleeping with 101 girls himself. He did so with an amazingly low attrition rate.

My thoughts were interrupted by the phone again. I was tired of the phone, but it was still a necessary evil for me.

"H h hey man, you go got a mmminute?"

"Yeah, what's up, Al?" I tried to sound normal. I was sitting at my desk supporting my head with my hand, eyes closed, wondering what my breaking point was going to be.

"I ju just wanted to to thhhank you for the o other day. Th that chick wa was really cool."

"Good, man, you deserve it. It was all you. Really." I actually felt good about that. It lasted about six seconds until reality settled back in and the damage I had done was far greater than overcoming someone else's speech impediment. But it was reassuring and I was hopeful that I could pull off a few more of those over the next few weeks while I figured everything else out.

Our conversation was not much longer than that. I hate reiterating it because of his stutter, but he was appreciative, I felt good about it, and I decided to keep giving these guys the best help that I could. Unfortunately for them, I still was not sure I was giving them good advice, I just knew I was giving them advice that they wanted. I wasn't going to get paid to be a new, moral me. I had to tell him what I know, and what he expects from me: She is cool, but don't stop there. You aren't going to be happy when you two get tired of each other. So prepare for the end of that one by beginning new relationships.

I didn't feel completely right about what I was telling him. But I promised that I was not going to go the cokehead route or the small-town vocational school girl route. So it was okay. I think.

CHAPTER 16

Lessons Learned

A lesson learned is worth two in the bush. I always liked the sound of that. There is no such thing as a complete failure; Girls will reject you, sometimes kindly, sometimes horrifically. If you view that as her fault, you are bound to make the same mistakes again and suffer the same consequences. In which case, you have failed.

Some lessons take longer to figure out. I made light of a case where I could not get an entire category of the female student body to sleep with me. I failed over and over until I finally realized that it was not me, it was how they saw me. It was through how I presented the same me from a different angle that I finally broke into this group.

I felt like I was learning all kinds of lessons lately, but they were not the kinds of things I ever wanted to learn. I didn't pursue this kind of knowledge. I guess in the long run I could say that these things are all a part of growing up. There is no prerequisite for how many deaths you have to be a part of to grow up. There aren't a set number of tragedies one must suffer to grow up.

> *T,*
> *Mom and Dad said its okay, and that this had to happen. It was part of the master plan. . .Oh, okay, that makes this fine. Thanks you two.*

I had an exam coming up in a global policies course. I didn't know much about it but there is a baseline level of what one needs to know to get by in that class. It is another class that is not hard, just cumbersome. I didn't do all of the reading but I did more than I ever had to date. This must be how fat people feel when they lose 10 pounds. 'Gosh, I may still be drastically bigger than I should, but this is pretty good for *me.*' I wasn't too worried about the exam either way. Enough of my professors are jaded academics who are too busy wondering what happened to their profession over the last few decades, and they are just grateful to fill a class on any given day. I think one guy gave extra credit my freshman year to anyone who showed up over half of the time.

Like I said. Middle of the road university. When you offer the same product that someone can get online for less than 1/5th of the cost and 1/20th of the pain there is bound to be a degradation here and there in the process. I don't know if that is in a book somewhere, but it seems pretty apparent by the day. Now that I am a little more involved in school, I have these weird opinions about stuff that never mattered to me. Not that I would ever get an online degree.

I woke up at the right time and had a cup of coffee. It would be a stretch to say that I was taking this stuff too seriously, but I think Chase was right. I needed a healthy distraction from my mess. I had a further distraction from that distraction in her, which I think removed me further from the mess. Time would tell that she led me right back to where I was without much of a detour.

I walked to my class bundled up in a peacoat, scarf, sweater and jeans. It was cold by my standards and I could never make it through autumn without getting deathly sick about three times from the change in weather. The sun came out and I cursed my shitty immune system.

The inside of the class was nice, compared to the ninth level of hell that I walked through to get in. That may have been a bit of an exaggeration, but it was going to hit those levels soon enough. Some of the fat kids were still wearing short sleeve shirts for god's sake. Those were more or less the extreme cases, but still. I was freezing my ass off and there was no acclimatization (check spelling) for me. Just clothing. I guess that was why I have always had a thing for good clothes. I required them. My logic has always been that if I have to have it, I want it to be good.

As students filled the room and the chatter got louder, I sat back and drank tea out of a thermos that I lugged along. I was never this awake at 7am but I was wry. I figured most of the lessons that I teach people translated well to everything and I was going to approach this exam like an Alpha male. Like someone who knew he was going to win when he walked onto the field. It couldn't have been that hard.

It wasn't that hard. It turns out that the 15 percent of the required reading I did actually helped. I never feared a word count or a page count because I had written a solid 30,000 words for my book, which came out to about 60 pages when written in essay form. This examination was to be four pages handwritten about something I vaguely knew. I also didn't have too much of a problem in the persuasion department. When the topic is handed to a moral relativist, the hardest part for him is picking which side to be on. I had 50 avenues on one side, and about 55 on the other. It really didn't matter either way because I was only going to pick one. What did my professor want to hear? That was the question.

I sat for about five minutes after the timer started. I drank my tea and thought about my prompt. I had to catch myself tapping a pencil. It was really someone else staring at me with a burning hatred that brought it to my attention. I put my hand up as to say 'I'm sorry', but it did no good. Someone under stress was going to exhibit that stress even when the catalyst was gone. It was a form of self-pity. I knew just by looking at him that that guy was totally fucked on this essay.

I figured out what I wanted to say and what I was going to use as evidence to say it. And then I did what everyone else did. I wrote frantically without stopping for about 35 minutes. My hand was cramping but I was done. I put it upside down on the front desk and left. It was still freezing out, but I could check one more thing off of my list of shit to take care of. And for someone like me, there were few things better than that.

I walked fast but without looking too hurried. I wasn't power walking, just trying to get to the warmth of my destination. It wasn't too far, but at 45 degrees outside anything was too far. There was only one thing that could have made the cold worse, but it wasn't raining, so I was sort of grateful. Not really, but I still made some mention of it in my inner monologue.

I don't know many of the details leading up to what happened next. I don't know how he found out, or what his initial reaction was. I don't know if this was planned or a savage reaction to something inevitable. I didn't get much of a warning, but I guess that part was fair, depending on your moral vantage point.

I felt a tug on my right shoulder. I turned around in time to see James reach back and punch me square on the cheek. I had never been hit before, but I was glad that it was a nerd who broke my cherry. I didn't hurt. Well, not the way I thought getting punched in the face would. It was more of a very blunt shock. I reacted by laughing. It was a shocked laugh, not a funny laugh, but he took it the wrong way.

"What the fuck are you doing?" I was half humored and completely fucking pissed that this guy just assaulted me.

"Me?! Me?! What the fuck did you do?! I trusted you!" Tears welled up. Most of my clients had been crying the last couple of days. "I fucking trusted you and you ruined it! Goddamn it, Tristan! Why can't I have something nice?" More sobbing.

"Look, Dude, I really don't know what you want me to say. I'm sorry. I'm sorry the world works the way it does. I wasn't helping you get her. I was helping you get all of them. Why the fuck don't you see that?"

I saw something inside of his head click. He looked at me like he had an epiphany, but didn't want to share it.

"I would kill you right now, T., I mean it. But you aren't fucking worth it."

He turned around to walk away. I didn't want to add insult to injury so I didn't inform him that since we were over he should pay me for the last month. I guess that is the problem with not drafting contracts. Although a contract might stipulate who I do and don't sleep with relative to my customer base. I would have to think about that one a little.

I went back to my place and looked at the damage. Nothing. I think there was a scuff on my cheek. It will probably be more obvious when I wake up tomorrow. I didn't really finish forming my thought before Stevo walked right in and laid down on my floor.

"I am so fucked up, T."

"You look like it, what have you been doing?"

"D-R-O-G-S. . ." I think I knew what he meant.

He fell asleep. I really didn't want to talk to him anyways, but I felt really uncomfortable with him lying there like that after the email I just got a couple of days ago.

CHAPTER 17

Dear Tristan,

I genuinely appreciate your submission and found there to be some real gems. I don't see work like that come across my desk very often. So thank you for the refreshing read.

The bad news, however, is that I could not convince my senior editor of its merit and while I am of a completely different opinion, my publisher is going to have to decline your book as it stands right now.

Don't take this to mean you should not keep trying. I included the URL to our website if you wish to have further guidance on publications, and strongly encourage you to make another go at it.

I wish you the best of luck in the future,

Joshua Diggins
Publication Editor

'Don't take this to mean that you should not keep trying'?! I wrote a fucking motivational book for the 21st century and this guy's fucking advice is to not give up. Thanks, Josh. Thank you so fucking much for your input.

I couldn't even see straight at the moment. I was growing tired of myself and my surroundings. I didn't have my own outlets anymore. I had given them up for my work. I dedicated myself to this and it was eating me alive. I could handle the burden of this or that, but not Robbie, and not Ash, and especially not with James jumping out of bushes and attacking me. I couldn't breathe, so to speak. I needed to find another outlet.

The first thing I did went contrary to every piece of advice that has ever been rationally given to someone who is not thinking clearly. I opened a beer and sat on my futon. I thought to myself for about 45 minutes about what I used to do for fun. I could sketch back in the day. I didn't care much for that after the first time I got laid. I guess the only thing I had really done to blow off steam was to work on my book over the last two years. The very thought of that book was enough to piss me off right now. I opened another beer.

I picked up my phone and scrolled down to C. C. dogg, C. Murder, Callie, Casey, Chase. Good, Chase. I hit call and thought to myself what I was going to say. But she answered before I could formulate something coherent.

"Hey, how are ya?"

"I'm good. I want to see you again. Your boyfriend attacked me and you owe me."

"My boyfriend?"

Why did she sound so confused?

"Uh, yeah." I was going to break my one rule for Chase: "James?"

"He's not my boyfriend. We went out like three times. He never even kissed me."

"I think he had a different idea. He punched me in the face today. What did you tell him?"

"Aw, you poor thing. Do you want to come over?" She sounded sincere. I needed sincere so I was all about it.

"Yeah, if that's okay. I didn't want to just barge in on you."

"Oh yeah, you are such a pain in the ass."

I'll go ahead and abbreviate the drive over and pick up the conversation again where it started.

"Come in, you look good considering you just got your ass kicked by a nerd." She laughed. I couldn't stand how much I liked her laugh. My day immediately seemed to brighten up.

What the hell was I doing? I don't say shit like that. My day began to brighten up?

"I really wanted to see you. I don't normally yearn to see a girl."

"Are you gonna tell me that you like me? Because you should have written me a note in social studies telling me so."

She hit me with a pillow that was sitting on her couch and jumped on top of me. We started to kiss. I would never turn this down, but I really needed to know what happened with James. If I knew one thing, it was that this is not the time or place to bring it up.

So I brought it up anyways.

"What was the deal with James?" Goddamn it. That just came out.

I should have kept my mouth shut. She climbed off, sat back and crossed her legs. She rested her head on her hand and gave me a very nonchalant look of 'whatever'. I was so busy trying to read her body language that I almost didn't hear what she said.

"He asked me out and I went out with him three times. We ate dinner three times and talked three times and I went home afterwards three times."

"What did you tell him about me?"

She looked like she felt sorry for him.

"He said that he wanted to take our relationship to the next level and I told him that I slept with you, so it wasn't really in the cards that we would be starting a relationship."

"Wait. He didn't even try to kiss you and after three dates he said he wanted to take this to the next level? Did he learn anything from me?!"

"Hum, I don't want to make this about me, but you seem mad that he didn't do more with me."

I was on a slippery slope here. The only person I felt like I could talk to was also the only person I didn't want to talk about my issues with. And by issues I mean the culmination of everything that resulted from me being me for the last few years.

"You're right, I'm sorry, it's just that I feel like I failed him." Obviously, I hate failure.

It was worse to fail someone than to betray him, because I knew that I wanted to sleep with Chase, but I didn't know that he paid me hundreds of dollars and all he got out of it was jogging a few miles and 'are you ready to go to first base with me now?'—I thought I was better than that.

Between that and my last email from a publisher, I was on the edge. I never really lost my shit, and I don't freak out and get very emotional, but I do stress out to the point of not eating or sleeping for days at a time. This is a semiannual occurrence and almost always correlates to changes in weather. If I knew any better I would diagnose myself with seasonal affected depression, but I am pretty sure that being responsible for a death, an unwanted baby and a life failure of sorts are not linked to the weather or the seasons. I can buy clothes for the weather, but for all of the advice I have, I could not figure out how to deal with certain things. Those things were coming to a head and I didn't know what the hell to do.

"Tristan, I can see that some things are bothering you. I know that you don't want to let down that masculine facade and let me in, but I'm sure that whatever problems you have are of your own doing. People like you are too smart not to create problems for themselves."

She was right. I am really smart. I guess somehow in finding everyone else's answers I always pushed my own aside.

"Is that written somewhere in the DSM?" I was going to use humor to get out of this one until I was ready to share my fucked up situation with her.

Also, the DSM is the Diagnostic and Statistical Manual for Mental Disorders. Most smart people know what it is. Welcome to the world of being smart.

"When you are ready, I am here to listen. I also think you should quit messing with all of these guys' heads and take care of yourself." I knew she was somewhat right, but that was a pretty big concession. I was not willing to talk about it either way.

"And until then," she continued, "if you are going to keep that cool facade on, why don't you come over here and show me how cool you really are."

Certain clothing items on each of us started to come off. We moved closer. More clothes off.

"Are you using me, Chase?"

"Yes."

Good enough for me.

CHAPTER 18

Obligations

There are really only a few obligations that one is held to. Those he holds himself to. When the necessities are taken care of (food, drink, a place to sleep), it all turns into a calculus of what is going to benefit him the most. No one wants to go to work, but being able to pay for things is necessary. No one wants to acquiesce to people that don't matter, but after doing it for one's boss, educators, the state and whoever else, it becomes a muscle memory to bend over for anyone who asks of it.

Ideally, this is the first habit a successful guy needs to break, but all bad habits are the first thing that a guy needs to break. If the opportunity does not present itself, create one for practice. Someone who is beholden to others is not just going nowhere, he is doing it at everyone else's pace.

While I sat in class, something I had been doing a lot more of lately, I tried to be patient, also something I have been doing a lot more of lately. I didn't approve of it, but I tolerated that mind numbing curricula. I tolerated the intrusion into my time, wallet and well-being. I didn't even mind when lecturers and professors pushed their politics on me. None of it mattered much, so I let it roll right off. What I did mind was that the one or two times to date that I cared about something they tried to drag it out and make it suspenseful. I just wanted my exam back from last week and that dick was holding onto it until the very last moment.

I had high hopes that I did well, based off of my own merit, whatever that is. I hoped so because if it was luck that I was dependent on then I was totally fucked. I don't really believe in luck *per se*, but I had overwhelming evidence stacking up by the day that there was such a thing as bad luck.

Life became *Bell Jar*-esque. I wasn't really happy this last week. I was happy enough when I went to Chase's apartment, but even when we were together I had this burning compulsion to tell her everything, and keeping that inside turned our time together into an emotional vice that was squeezing my temples.

I almost slept through the morning lecture. I couldn't reiterate three words of it if I had to. I just wanted my damn test results and I wanted to leave. I was chewing on my pen and spacing out when the same kid who got pissed at me during the exam caught my eye with his death-stare. I had been tapping my foot. Oops. Fuck that guy. Sorry, though. I went back to my daydreaming, and I presume captain asshole death-stare guy could focus again on agrarian influence over blah blah blah politics in blah blah blah country.

The time eventually came and a TA sat in the front calling out names and handing out exams. Mine finally landed on my desk, in that I had someone else get it for me, and I was pleasantly surprised to find that I knew what I was talking about. More likely it was that I knew how to talk about something I didn't know anything about. Either way, I could be satisfied with my A. My shiny, new A. Those weren't always so foreign to me. But of late, they were not only foreign, but also welcomed. One might even say 'earned'.

The pride in my achievement wore off and I got up to leave. It was nice to feel good about something for five minutes, but I had bigger fish to fry. Today was my day to talk to Alex, Taylor and James. You can imagine that I would not be talking to James for one reason or another. But I scheduled the other two for the same day so that I could get our meetings over with for the week and not worry about it. I wanted to keep it short and vague. I didn't want to hear them do much talking, although there was a requisite amount of shit that I was going to have to listen to. I figured I would give them each about five minutes to share, five minutes to listen and a minute to explain that 'something came up and hey, this was a good chat, but I gotta go. What we covered should be sufficient until next week'.

It was a good plan, but from the time the first shot was fired, my plan went to hell. Alex left me a message during class and told me that today was bad, and that tomorrow was the only day he could see me. I normally don't bend to other guys' schedules, but I was so burnt out this week that I just accepted it. I told myself not to make this a habit. I liked the way I said it so when I returned his call I said the same thing.

"And Alex. . ."

"Yeah, Tr Tristan?"

"Don't make this a habit."

Taylor was noon to 12:30. We were going to meet in person, which was contrary to his way of doing things and contrary to what I felt like. So it fit perfectly into the theme for the week: Fuck What Tristan Wants. . .with the glaring exception of my huge success on that exam. I crushed it and I was the only person who told me what a good job I did.

I had about two hours until I would see Taylor, so I occupied myself by jotting down notes about my plan. I didn't have an end goal. Yet.

It seems like a counterintuitive way to set the bar for oneself, but I needed to oil my engine. I needed to stretch my intellect a little further than stupid papers about industrialism and social tides. The plan was more like a way to conduct myself until I had another sustainable goal. The old goals, the book, the work, the 200th girl all came into question. Not because of Chase harping on my lifestyle, but it sure as hell didn't help. I wasn't necessarily giving those up, but I was questioning them, and if I was doing that then I ran a huge risk of being inconsistent with my clients. That was completely against my way of doing things, so I needed a plan for them. I don't give them my goals, but I use my paradigm for their goals. That wasn't working lately, so

I had to do something. That paradigm was where everything came from.

I had nothing. Almost two hours had passed and nothing worthwhile had come to me. Yet. I put a sweater on followed by my jacket, a scarf, a pair of sunglasses and an adequate pair of shoes. The cold outside today was more biting than it had been and I was preparing for the long haul. I took a vitamin C chewable to be on the safe side and left for Angie's.

I say things about how right I am all the time. I always point out that I hit the nail on the head, even when it is an understatement. I am not shy about being so unequivocally on point and I need to take a moment to describe the cold. The scarf was a nice touch, and even the glasses shielded my eyes from the freezing wind. I cut the trip in half by power walking and ignoring passers-by. In a short matter of the worst five minutes I had experienced since finding out that I was a killer, I was inside Angie's and two minutes ahead of Taylor. I had just ordered a cup of hot tea, a water-no ice, and a veggie pizza when I turned around to see something I could not immediately comprehend: Taylor was standing in the doorway dressed like a bro.

I want to assume you know what I mean by 'bro' when I say it. But to spare us the risk of miscommunication I will give it a stab.

Taylor wore a flat brimmed hat, slightly cocked to the side. He had a puffy jacket and a *faux* diamond earring. He had other jewelry, Adidas shoes and baggier than normal pants. I suddenly realized that I had not seen him in over two months and I had no idea how long he had been parading around dressed like a fucking bro, carrying my ideals around in those big pockets and in that puffy jacket.

As I said before, you can dress up. You can work out. You can gel your hair, wear jewelry and cologne, but if you don't know even the most basic psychology you will not go half as far as you are capable. In Taylor's case, you won't even get laid. And he wasn't.

"Tristan, what's up?"

"Hey, man, first of all," I paused. I didn't know what to say. Should I try now, or figure this out? Fuck it. I will wait.

"Yeah?"

"Oh, nothing. I was about to ask about something that had nothing to do with you."

"Was it about James?"

God. Damn. It.

If I had complete control over the world, I would keep everyone I knew apart. *Divide et impera*. But if you have already conquered, dividing is just an administrative convenience. I often forget that plenty of these guys know each other. I work off of references so it is no shock that word travels in certain circles at light speed. Fortunately for me, shame keeps those circles small and enclosed. Loose lips sink chances of Tristan helping you become better—i.e., getting laid—in so many sad cases.

"It's cool with me, man. A bitch is a bitch is a bitch."

I couldn't believe what I was hearing. I am not easy to offend, but bitch is a word to describe wimpy guys, when someone is being incredibly abrasive. As a person who is certainly not moral by any definition I just don't use that word. It makes one sound too much like those guys who wear flat brimmed hats and puffy jackets.

"There is more to it than that, Taylor." I sounded patronizing, but Taylor was acclimated enough to being low man on the totem pole, so he took the tone well. "I don't feel like talking about it, but it is not nearly as dramatic as you think."

"Like I said, man. . ."

Fuck this guy. What the hell was he doing? I really thought I was better than that. How many people have I ruined?

"I gotta go, man. Call me next week. We need to work something else out."

I walked away.

"Tristan, what about the pizza?"

"It's yours. I'm not hungry."

I was starving, but I was also glad to stick him with the bill, the whole pizza and a lunch by himself. It was time for me to go back and start working on that plan again. I began to really formulate. Something was on the horizon.

CHAPTER 19

Letting Her Off Smoothly

There are so many ways to let a girl down. It is much better to start a tryst, one-night stand or short relationship with complete honesty, but in the event that you just can't, you need to be a gentleman when you tell her the truth. The truth can come wrapped in parcel paper made of lies and tied together with little lies, but ultimately, it has to be the truth. Never say you are going to call if you are not going to call.

If you say you don't plan on calling because you are being sent by the CIA to the Colombian jungle to hunt down some guerillas, then at least she won't wait by the phone. There is a grain of truth. No one gives a shit about your reason. The whole point of a reason is to make you feel better for being a pussy who couldn't state his intentions in the first place.

Try to be nice about it. Try to start out with honesty and if that goes to hell, then at least have the courtesy to make a smooth exit.

I was in my room. I was pacing back and forth and tossing a tennis ball from one hand to the other. I had a notebook on my desk, and would occasionally sit to jot something and get up to pace again. This was a normal way of thinking for me. What made it slightly different this time was the bourbon on the desk. I had a bottle of tonic water and ice and was on my second glass.

Alcohol was never my thing. I don't love it and I quit

drinking much of it after about three months of college. I use it on especially bad days. I never had too many of those, but I like to fall back on something so basic. It is not a solution, but an amazing tool for self-pity. And since I cannot let other people know when I am going through bouts of self-pity, drinking by myself is a great way to deal with that.

My handwriting was getting noticeably sloppier, but I was still in the right frame of mind. I decided that working with individuals wasn't good anymore; there were too many mistakes I could make. My idea, my epiphany, was that I needed to try a group seminar. I needed a 'method.' I needed a set of rules and guideposts and I wouldn't have to take credit for assholes like Taylor.

I looked at the bottle. I figured I had a good excuse to do anything I wanted. I picked up my phone and did what I wanted. It rang a few times and I got a "Hello?"

"Do you want to do something?"

She sounded game.

"And what might that be?"

"Can I tell you the truth? Or should I pretend something else?"

"Truth."

"I want to fuck you, stupid." I was trying to sound sober, but I don't think I sounded like me either way.

"I will see you soon, Tristan."

In the meantime, I sat down at my computer. I think Chase was going to appreciate that I used it. I brought up my email and re-read my last rejection. It was that Josh Diggins bastard who tried to encourage me to follow my dreams, in spite of his rejection of them.

"What about my dreams, you fucking prick?" Talking to myself was a side effect of the booze.

I hit reply and went to work. Of course, I did so only after I had another drink. I don't love bourbon, but I love that it gets easier with every sip. And when mixed with a shot of tonic water, I was chugging it by my fourth.

To whome it may concenr,

I recently submitted a book for publication that apparently did not meet some standsar that you claim to have at your publisher. I ferequent many bookstores and can tell you now that for the amont of shit that people put out there these days it says somethiung aobut a writer who cannot get his book printed. If youfeel so storongly about it then I would appreciate if you came to my house and told my to fuck off rather than send your email saying "keep trying".
Fuck you and the hosre you rode inon.

Tristan Algren

I really let the bourbon do the talking. I don't have an 'angry' drink. There isn't one that really gets me, but bourbon apparently brought out the me that I was hiding. It made me brutally honest. If I was happy, it made me brutally happy. Today, it made me brutally jaded.

I proofread it and it seemed fine, given I was on my fifth drink.

SEND.

Done.

I was just in time for a power nap before a long carnal night. Anyone who drinks whiskey knows what I am talking about. That feeling that if you just lay down for a minute you will be good later. Regardless of what happens every time one lies down after five drinks in an hour's time.

My wakeup was rough. I had apparently only been out for about 15 minutes when she let herself in and jumped on top of me. I wasn't in the mood by that point. But I tried. I hate to waste an opportunity. We started to kiss and it was not long at all before I had a beautiful, topless girl straddling me and pulling my shirt off.

"You don't look so good, Tristan."

We sat there looking at each other for a second. It may have been longer, I don't know, because I had no clue which way was up.

"I'll be fine. These things work themselves out." Every word was a labor not to slur. I spoke about 1/3 of my normal tempo just to make myself understood. I had one eye closed so there were only two breasts in front of me. I laughed because there were four when I tried to focus.

"I don't think you're really up to the challenge." She poked a very limp me through my jeans. "You just may be over your head this time."

I stared at her for a moment. In my drunken stupor, I tried to shirk off what it meant to me, which was clearly different than what she meant by it. She was obviously talking about what wasn't going to happen for the next few hours. And as the room spun around my head, in my head spun ideas about my failures, mishaps and bleak horizon. I changed the subject in my inner monologue and marched forward with the business at hand.

"I can do this." I didn't know if I was completely coherent, but I knew I wasn't smooth. "Don't give up on me, Chase."

She stared at me. She slowly climbed off and put her shirt back on. I was confused and she must have sensed it, because she explained:

"I'm Laura, you asshole."

"Laura?"

"Yeah, Laura."

There was no turning back at this point. No smooth talking was going to put out this fire. It was a lost cause for about three seconds when I decided to make a bonsai charge for one last request that sounded infinitely better than bourbon laden, fumbling, tired sex.

"Can I have a glass of water, Laura?"

And wouldn't you know it, that sweetheart went into my kitchen and got me a glass of water. While I waited, I closed one eye again and tried to keep the room from spinning. It didn't work and I tried closing both. That also failed. Nausea set in, but I kept it down. I was not the prince charming that completely rocked this girl's world a week or so ago. I was his polar opposite and losing ground fast.

"I know you are going to pay for this all day tomorrow, Tristan, so I don't feel too bad." She handed me the cup and pet my leg.

"Thank you for the water." I was talking like a little kid does when he is sick. Slow, forced, theatric almost.

"Bye, Tristan." It sounded like we could still be friends.

I was going to have to send her a card or some flowers. I would have liked to stay higher in her esteem because she is always going to have a special place on my bedpost and I would remember that forever.

She wasn't mad. Looking back, I think she knew that I was no good for the night when she saw me passed out. I like that she tried. I appreciate self-starters in my line of work. I always meant to apologize somewhere down the road.

I looked at the notebook I had been brainstorming in. All very good notes. I flipped a few pages, ripped one out and wrote, "Call Laura. Say Sorry". That would do. I left it where I could see it and got up to brush my teeth.

Before I made it to the bathroom, I got back on the kick where I wanted to do whatever I want. And I wanted to tell Chase everything. So I picked up my phone and called.

Her voicemail answered, so I began in my attempt at a sober voice:

"It's Tristan. I want to say to you. . ." Okay, shit. This was not going in the right direction. "I want to tell you everything, K? Alright, so if there's time, call me, okay? I'm gonna be here, but sleeping maybe, so bye."

I really regrouped and saved myself towards the end. I regretted that I wasn't more of a drinker in that it would have been nice to articulate better after five or six glasses of bourbon. But, oh well.

I brushed my teeth as long as I could stand and drank

some more water. I took three vitamin C pills and lay down. In another attempt to keep the room from spinning I tried to focus on something, so I recounted the whole night before completely passing out in my clothes.

Epiphany. Bourbon. Nap. No sex with girl who was not Chase. Email to publisher. Message. Vitamin C.

At least I brushed my teeth.

CHAPTER 20

Voicemail: Call.

Hey, Asshole, it's Stevo. Call me. There are going to be about twenty whores at my place this weekend. There are also going to be felony portions of the best narcotics and a screening of Timmy's short film. Spoiler: It sucked dick, but it should be fun celebrating anyhow. Call. Call. Call.

I was pretty haggard when I woke, but not defeated. My head did hurt and I hung up the phone with a melodramatic "Fuck! My head. . ." I just needed something to eat and Paradise was the order of the day. It was Tuesday and I didn't have any classes until 11. I had plenty of time to eat, hydrate and start making some decisions. Calling Stevo back was not one of them. I hadn't talked to him or Timmy in about three weeks, and even though I knew it was going to be longer before I did, I felt reassured for a moment that people still wanted to be around me.

The first decision I wanted to make was obvious to me. I had been desperate to talk about what I had done and there was only one person I could do that with. I didn't mean the Laura thing, that was going to stay with me. I didn't know when I would see Chase again, but after I set my mind to it, it was imperative that we talked. I was already ruining what we had together by stressing about something that I wouldn't even share. If I was driving her away anyhow, what difference did it make that she left me because I have baggage and I am not fun, or because I am a semi-murderer. Chase needed to find out the truth. Minus the whole Laura thing.

I was now almost completely convinced that I played a part in a death. I hadn't heard any more from Ash's mom; the point hadn't been driven home by an angry mob or a barrage of one-sided arguments. I had just thought about it more and more until I believed it. I probably would not have bought into it under other circumstances, but in light of my other recent failures, it was easier to believe that I was capable of royally fucking up like this. I didn't know how to own it because I didn't deal with shit like that. Was I supposed to call his family and apologize? There were so many questions I had about being a normal, functional, average member of society. Chase would have the insight. I hoped.

I put a lot of stock in her because I liked her. I liked a lot of girls, but she made me feel something completely different. She was girlfriend material. She was yet to prove that she had all the answers, but I assumed she had some just because without even knowing all of my circumstances she had called me out on my M.O. That does not happen to me much and I liked it. Eventually I spent a good deal of time idealizing her into the wise nerd that I was falling for little by little. If someone else said the same things she said, I would be much less apt to agree.

Paradise Café was nearly empty. I walked in and got my table. I ordered a slightly bigger than normal breakfast with a few extra greasy items that fit the bill for the hangover, which I was slowly defeating. I drank orange juice although I had about 1400% of my vitamin C the night before in pill form. The toast, bacon and eggs were exactly what I needed to get that sloshing feeling out of my stomach. If this was Paradise, then my waitress was a divorcée, a 45-year-old angel. The angel of toast and bacon and dissipating hangovers.

After I talked to Chase I was going to wing it. There was nothing else to know if I didn't know what conclusions we were going to arrive at together. I became focused on what I thought might happen, but the truth was, at that point, I didn't even know when I was going to see her again. I wanted to. I almost had to, now, just because of how I built it up in my head. I knew that she would say to study more and do well in school, but that was a given. I had to do that anyhow, with or without her advice.

"Here you go, honey." My waitress handed me another orange juice. "You look like you could use it." She smiled and I thanked her. Angel. No other way to put it.

I always liked the women here. Most of them were older. None of them students. There was no compulsion for me to hit on, sleep with or exploit them. They were always nice to me and it just felt homey going to Paradise.

I saw a familiar face and we nodded to each other. None of the regulars really spoke. A few might exchange a word here or there, but it wasn't some barbershop where everyone knew everyone else's business. The waitresses were an exception to that rule, but it was kind of their job to be like family to these old guys who came here alone to read the paper and drink that abysmal coffee. I looked at one of them, sitting there, eating his breakfast alone. I wondered if he had slept with 100 girls. Probably not, but he was young during the 70's, so maybe. I wondered if he killed anyone like I did, be it circuitous or drug related. But, then again, he was young in the 70's, so maybe.

I finished my OJ and left a 20 on the table. My reputation as a tipper was well known, but today I outdid even myself. If there was karma, I was going to get some. Realistically, I think I had another million or so to tip before the good kind catches up with me.

I walked home completely quiet. I felt down, obviously. The headache was gone, but I created a muscle memory, a chemical memory in my brain for just being down and out. I still had a shitload of cash saved, I had all of the material things I wanted, for the most part, and I had a phone full of numbers that I could call for great sex at a moment's notice. Most of my 'peers' would kill for my situation. It turns out that I did, in fact.

Stevo walked up from behind me and caught me off guard while I was sulking my way back to my room. I wanted some more solitude and I still had an hour before class, so every second he spoke I felt like forever. He was talking about one of three things: booze, coke or sluts. I didn't care much for any of those at the moment and I tuned him out and just kind of waited for him to finish. I heard something about Taylor.

"Wait, what, Stevo?"

"You know? That guy you hung out with a couple of months ago? The one who wore that vest to a party. He got the beer thrown at him. You know?"

That was definitely him. I think his reception at that party was even harsh for someone who was outcast. Someone threw a beer at him so he would take it off after repeatedly saying that he would rather not and then he spent the rest of the night hiding behind his beer. To his credit, he stuck with his guns. It was very Taylor of him. To his detriment, he stuck to his guns over some pretty stupid bullshit. Also, very Taylor of him. I always assumed that was why he would always rather just talk over the phone. Apparently, he needed someone to hold his hand and tell him how not to be a tool. I wasn't there for him.

"Hey, man, what the hell is your problem?" His tone changed from constant chatting to concerned.

"What do you mean?" I asked. I already knew what he was going to say.

"You just seem out of it, I just asked you two questions and you are staring at me. Are you on something?" Okay, not exactly what I thought he was going to say. "So after he got his ass kicked, instead of running off, he fucking stayed for one more beer, and that bitch he was with left with him. It was epic. I don't know what happened to him, but he is a tenacious fucker."

I wanted to be proud, but I felt nothing but disgust. The way he dressed and acted, it didn't matter if he was sleeping with some sorority chick. He was on par with about 85 percent of the sexually active students on campus. Not better. Maybe not worse. Just par for the course.

Stevo must have seen that I was anxious to go because he rolled his eyes at me and told me to call sometime, when I wasn't busy. I think he was pouting. I was never a friend people pout to, but I felt something this time. I was taking it personally that he was taking it personally.

I thought for a second. "It's school, dude. I have class soon, but I'll call you later." I realized immediately that it sounded like an excuse. It was.

"That shit can be bad for you, T. Don't do too much of it. It can replace your friends pretty quickly if you aren't careful."

I think that is what his parents told him about drugs. At least he remembered what they said.

He seemed pissed. I stood there for a second thinking a million miles an hour about the repercussions of alienating one of my so-called friends. None of them was good. Then again, neither was I. I needed to get out of this slump before it completely ruined the rest of college for me.

It dawned on me that I had other friends, who paid me a lot more than Stevo, who I owed a minute of my time. I wanted to do something before I forgot about it, again, and I called Dustin.

"Hello?"

"How are you holding up?"

"Oh, hey, man. I guess I'm alright. It took about a week to wrap my mind around what was going on, but I can't do anything about it now, can I?"

"No, man, I guess you can't." I had to think for a second. I don't have these talks often. People have looked to me for some pretty lofty things, but solace was never one of them. "I'm sorry how things turned out, dude."

"Nothing you can do. Where have you been, anyways? We were supposed to get together last week, but you never answered your phone. I figured you were out of town or something."

"Yeah, I was. Personal stuff. I guess we can make a time soon. I have to figure some things out, but I will get back to you."

"Okay. Have a good one."

He hung up and I stood there for about two minutes. I didn't have to figure out a scheduling conflict. I had to figure out what the fuck I was going to do.

CHAPTER 21

Tenacity

The ability to cut your losses will lead to much more success than trying to be some human-interest story who stuck with some menial goal and almost achieved it after 100 tries. It is cute, but real life would not be worth living if you spent a college career trying to be on the football team and ended up with a whole 30 seconds of play. Just imagine the inefficiency of success if all things were so hard-gotten. Make a note of this, Algren.

I made it a whole week without really talking to anyone. Anyone but Chase. The problem was that I never talked to her about what I really wanted to. I completely pussed out of my decision to open up. It's ironic to puss out of something that makes you a bigger pussy. I should really rethink my phrasing.

She told me that I seemed really down lately. I had been. She was the one person I tried to hide it from. If she knew something was up, then everyone else who I interacted with must have thought I was going to kill myself. We spent two nights together and didn't even kiss. I was beginning to overthink the whole thing. Now I know how all of those other guys felt when they talked about girls that they were really into.

I wasn't really depressed as much as I was just average for the first time in my adult life. Average for me was worse than being depressed, because average means that it doesn't matter if said person is sad or not. Average has no more of a right to feel sad than anyone else. Average people are everywhere and their feelings don't matter as much. They stay in the middle and I was just on the low side of the middle. I broke my several years streak of being on top. Feeling normal felt like having a bad cold. It just sucked, and I hated it. I didn't try to be the center of rooms that I walked into. I didn't respond to emails from two more potential clients. And the worst part was, at that point, I figured I was doing them a favor.

I showed up to all of my classes and when I walked between them I thought of my life in terms of a montage to a really emo acoustic song. I saw myself walking to this song between classes and sitting there, bored while professors talked. I saw me doing schoolwork and getting coffee alone. I saw myself getting rejection after rejection from fucking publishers who didn't like my book.

I wondered to myself how Nietzsche got published. He said some things that really offended the sensibilities of the 19th century. So did Marquis de Sade. *The Satanic Verses* is still in print and I couldn't publish a book about how to improve your life without the usual bullshit rigmarole. What was missing? What was it that they had that I didn't? An agent? An editor at $5 a page for 160 pages? I wasn't going to go that far. I used to thrive off of the challenge. Now I felt worse by the day.

It was a Wednesday afternoon. The wind chilled the already cold 40 degrees by another five or so and I was bundled up. I was hell-bent on not getting sick anytime soon, based purely on the fact that my body just might completely stop functioning if I physically felt how I emotionally felt. I was ambling from a lecture on the Reagan Era, trying to forget everything I had just learned, when I saw him.

James was right in front of me, He was also walking by himself and his demeanor was not as confident as it had been the last few times I saw him. Hopefully he would not try to replay our last encounter. One, because I didn't want to take my hands out of my jacket pockets to defend myself and lay him out. And two, because I really didn't want to get punched in the face by a nerd. There were more people around this time and if I got a black eye from someone of a lower social stature, it would have consequences. I kept telling myself that one off-season from the parties and girls would not kill my reputation. But when we add in a few fights with a guy designing a video game, I start to lose credibility.

As Murphy's Law would have it, he turned around. I didn't act surprised, I was, but I didn't show it and just said "Hey."

He said it back and had a look that indicated he was searching for something else to say.

I stopped to entertain his whim.

"Why, man?"

It was the best he could do, and as I said, I was going to entertain him.

"She chose me. It wasn't I, it wasn't you. It was Chase. She probably just wanted someone to make a move." I didn't know how he would take it. The words just came out like that and I hoped I didn't sound too abrasive.

"Yeah, maybe. You don't go from being like me to being like you overnight, Tristan."

It sounded pathetic, but I realized how true and sad it was for every single guy that I sold my help to. I had to think for a second but it came to me.

"She didn't want you to be like me. She wanted you and you didn't give it up."

That was not actually true. I was lying, but it was kind of working. He looked disarmed. I could tell at that moment he wasn't going to assault me. I felt more relaxed, and was interested in what I had to say.

"I don't date girls that don't put out, why would they not feel the same about a guy?" As I said it, it looked like a light bulb went off in his head. I really should have charged him for this, but I guess it was gratis. A freebee for the price of one completely hot stolen girlfriend.

"Hold on, say that again."

I could tell he was really interested. I knew instantly that this was the missing piece he had been looking for, suffering over for the last couple of weeks. I wished my missing piece would come to me this easily. If only there were a few more people like me walking around so that people like me had others to gain guidance from.

"I said girls like sex too. They obviously need a certain set of preconceived notions to be met and anything you can do to make it seem ideal and romantic is even better. But girls don't hate sex, James, so don't go around avoiding it and calling that chivalry."

I wanted to explain Chase as a case in point. I decided against it as a matter of tact, but the words were somewhere on the tip of my tongue.

It hit me that I taught him so much about confidence and meeting new people that I didn't teach him anything about the endgame. I touched on the ethics of being like me, but I never gave him more than that.

I think he wanted to do something with that brightly shining light bulb above his head, because he was quick to acknowledge what I said, say goodbye and scurry off. I could tell by the way he carried himself that he got back into running. He had a more solid gait, and slightly more coordination than most other guys who spent too much time on computers. I guess I could take some credit for that.

Maybe I should just become a certified personal trainer.

The rest of my walk back to my place was wrought with questions. I had this small sense of confidence about the good that I am capable of. A guy who hated my guts came to me looking for conflict and I answered questions he didn't even ask. If that is not a talent then nothing really is. I also felt like I was on a slippery slope giving out advice. I would have been gun shy if someone just came out and asked me for my input on something. But since what I said just came out I did not hesitate. I did have a talent. I would waste it if I did nothing but study and become more of the person that Chase wanted me to be.

There must have been something in the air where I lived. Or associative psychology was real and I felt an overwhelming sense of unease when I walked inside. I was back to where I was at that morning. There was no hope of possibly rekindling things. There didn't seem to be any real chance that I would be any better at my advocacy practice after a tragedy. I could make logical cases in my head all day long, but I could not convince myself that I was any better for what happened. I don't subscribe to the old-fashioned lesson learning, get-back-on-the-pony bullshit. Life is not long enough. If something fails, and you are not in fact the star of some fictitious, underdog story, then odds are that was not your forte, but fuck it, don't cut your losses. Find what world you belong in. Inhabit your world. But if you kill someone in the course of telling him how to live, then you should quit selling your advice.

That belongs on a fortune cookie.

CHAPTER 22

There are times when it is perfectly okay to cut and run:
— When a girl's boyfriend comes home to catch you in bed with her;

— When you find a cache of pills in a girl's bathroom that indicate a certain level of instability (more than the normal amount of instability one should expect from the female genus);

— When you discover a girl is not yet old enough to vote;

— And then there are countless others.

The idea of calculated loss applies to so much more than girls. The main reason they are the emphasis of this chapter is that most guys have no problems cutting their losses and moving on when it comes to everything. Everything except pussy. Most guys who didn't have a steady supply in the first place can't just walk away from a willing girl. So often, however, it is necessary.

Let me say that again: It is necessary. Period.

I have never had a problem taking that advice. I could always walk away. What is hard for me is letting go of clients. Taylor was obviously a piece of cake to say goodbye to. He was a fuckhead if I ever knew one, and I wish there was nothing linking the two of us. Fortunately for me, he is not going to readily admit that he paid me for advice on how to dress, socialize, and meet girls. And whether or not he did pay me for that stuff then, he is on his own path now. I don't think I have had any real influence on his vocabulary, his style or his choice of friends.

Dustin and Alex, on the other hand, were going to be much harder to say goodbye to. I wanted to help Dustin more than most, especially with all of the shit he was going through. I guess could just be a friend to him, but I always thought I was a worse friend than I was a Life Coach, and my coaching was the bane of my, and several other existences. It goes without saying that I was not really going to be a good friend anyhow, but with all of the shit I had going on, there is no way I really felt bad that his parents were a statistic. I think the only good advice I had for him, in my assessment, was that he should pit them against each other more, and play off of it. I had friends growing up who completely milked their parents' divorces. It is never too late to show them that emotional damage is not free. I thought about telling him this, but with my recent string of luck, such advice would end in a murder/suicide.

Al was another one who deserved better than I did. He was one of the few guys who was at a natural disadvantage that I really thought should get a better chance. For him to overcome my emotional block towards empathy, and to overcome my sense of Darwinism in the social sense was really an amazing feat that he didn't even know he overcame. I would have liked to say something, but I don't think he would have taken it as much of a compliment.

So there I was, after having mastered the morning-after talk, the "let's just be friends talk", I was stressing about how to tell these dudes that I was not the right guy for them. Breaking up is so hard to do. I figured I would give their money back, for pre-paid sessions that were never going to happen, but the one thing I didn't know is what I would tell them. I could not come out and tell the truth: I am a semi-killer and a terrible life coach. From Al's perspective I was golden and I know Dustin had no complaints. They were inevitably going to ask 'why?' and I didn't have a 'why' to tell them. I had to come up with something.

"Fuck it."

I called Dustin and took a deep breath. I hated myself for

what I was doing.

Voicemail: "Dustin, hey. It's Tristan. I had to talk to you about a few things. So when you get a chance, gimme a call back. Thanks."

God damn it. Of course he wasn't there. It was mid after-noon. He and 4000 other people at this school were in classes right now. I guess Al is going to be doing the same thing. But I hadn't spoken to him in quite a while, so I owed it to him to at least call and leave a message. I actually owed him about 200 dollars' worth of service. Beginning with a phone call that was a week or two overdue.

"Hey, Tristan. I th th thought you died. Where ha have you b b been?"

"Out of town." Since I hadn't been out much it was a to-tally believable piece. "I meant to catch ya and tell you we had to re-schedule, but I think it's more complicated than that. Can we meet up soon?"

"Yea yea yeah. Sure. When?"

"Tomorrow is good for me. Is lunch at 11 okay?" I re-membered a time when that meant I got to shine and try to improve humanity. Now it meant saying goodbye.

"I'll be there." A moment passed where something oc-curred to both of us at the same time. "Where?" he added on.

"Harvey's." A local burger joint, close to campus.

"Ah alright, Tristan. 11 o'clock."

So there I had it. I had set my second to the last date as a life coach. There was never a time when I had to recant my system. I have taken back individual mistakes twice in my life. I cannot remember both of them, but I do know that I have, at some point, gone back on something to fix it. I was only nearly perfect. Not perfect. Now I was something completely different. I didn't know what to call it. Fucked up. Incomplete. Sad.

The day went by like so many others recently. I studied, did some schoolwork and in an attempt not to go out and talk to anyone or do anything, I cleaned my place. It was kind of cathartic to me to just listen to music and tidy up. I didn't do it often enough, so at the end of the night I felt like I had finally done something good. It was the first time in a couple of weeks that I felt something like that. Pathetic.

The next morning came fast and 11am came just as quickly. I drove over to Harvey's and gleaned over a newspaper while I waited for Al. I took a good look around and there were only about three people in there, no noteworthy girls, though.

Al walked in five minutes early and sat down with me.

"What's up?"

"No no nothin."

"I don't know how to do this. I've never done it before, so, here." I put 200 dollars on the table. And then, just as I predicted:

"Why?" He left it there. It hurt to look at. Not that parting with 200 dollars meant anything to me. I was wearing a pair of 180-dollar jeans. Even now, cash was not a problem, it was that I was giving up the most gratifying thing I had ever done.

"I am up to my neck in shit that I don't have time to take care of."

"Oh. I guess you do do don't owe me an e e explanation."

"No, I really do." I wanted to tell him the truth. I never cared about anything except saving face, but when someone is weakened, he reverts to more humble values. I was a victim of western conditioning, and the Sunday school lessons I had drilled into me when I was little were trying to come out. I wasn't going to give up that easily. "I just need to work on graduating. I spent too much time on one area of my life and now I need to get the others up to speed before I fuck myself."

"You could ha have told me on th th the phone."

"I think you are one of the smartest guys I have helped and I wanted to give you this month's money back."

"Well, wh what about summer?"

"Yeah, man. I may be around this summer. I would love to develop some new material this summer and maybe I can do more for you."

Sometimes we say what sounds ideal and not what is

real. I was doing it now. It was just easier.

"Is that all?"

"Yeah." I noticed that when he was mad his stutter subsided.

He stood up. "I guess I'll talk to you this summer."

I felt like a total shithead as he walked out.

"Al," he turned around. "Keep on the track you are going. You may not even need me this summer."

Parting words. They drew the attention of the dude sitting closest to us. I guess out of context that was an interesting thing to hear.

"Sure."

As he left, our waitress walked up.

"Will you be dining alone?"

"Yes. Alone."

Breaking up is hard to do.

CHAPTER 23

Feelings

Suppress them. Hide them. Deny them. Hate them. Bury them. Did I say suppress them yet? Do whatever it takes. They will lead you down paths that you do not want to go. They will burn marks on your soul, and they will crush whatever sense of self you have.

Feelings are not you; they are what your church and your mommies and daddies and all of your teachers told you to feel about certain things. This is their way of controlling you, even when they are not around. You can try to take them into account all day long, but when the cards fall, they will be your ruin.

Jeremy called a few days ago and I completely blew him off. It wasn't one of those things where you see later that you missed a call and don't return it. I ignored the ringing phone because I didn't want to talk. I wanted to, but not to any of my 'friends'. Also, not to Chase. Or my counselor. Or my family. Who else was there? At this point, the most reasonable thing to do would have been to get a journal but there was no way in hell that I was going to leave evidence behind that I had these. . .feelings. If that is what you would even call them.

I guess the biggest problem that I had was that there was no real Tristan-way of going about this problem, 'this problem' being the life ruining/ ending that my *life advocating* practice had led to or the shitty grades that I was suffering as a result from my immense focus on others' well-being. Not that I actually achieved anything close to their well-being. Now I was between a rock, a death, a Marine, a poli-sci class, and my first failing relationship. It doesn't take a military strategist to see that I fucked myself into an unwinnable conflict. This was the conflict; the bombs were the feelings that kept broadsiding me and the bullets were the incessant phone calls from people I could not really talk to.

I called Jeremy. I didn't want to talk, but I still felt this compunction to maintain my few friends. The ones that didn't pay me. Stevo was less a friend and more of a liability, a fun liability, so I had no qualms about letting him slowly slip, but Jeremy was a slightly more normal and stable friend.

'Friend.'

His ringtone was that Plain White T's song. The one about the girl. I wanted to vomit. I liked the song, but *no* guy says so out loud, and no guy makes that his ringtone.

"Hey, Tristan, I thought you were dead."

"Nope; dying, but not there yet."

"What's going on?"

"I have just been so buried in school and all this other bullshit that I haven't had much me-time."

"I know what you mean. Amber is freaking out about her finals in like a month, and her mother actually called me the other day to talk about wedding stuff, and here I am trying to get ready for finals."

I used to think it was unforgivable that he couldn't open his mouth without uttering 'Amber', but I got used to it. Now that I have (had?) Chase, I kind of knew where he was coming from. . .And then his words hit me:

"Holy fuck! You are getting married!?"

"No, not yet at least. I never asked, it was just something her mother assumed was coming soon, so she wanted to 'touch bases' as she put it. It freaked me out a little. I don't know what to do. I thought about asking this summer, but now it feels forced. How is everything with your chick, Chase? Right?"

"Yeah, Chase. We have both been so busy, you know?" It sounded like an excuse. I know what those sound like. I never really used them before. But I hear them all the time from clients.

"Well, you need to get not busy. That chick is hot. You would be a fucking idiot to ignore her for your bullshit projects. A friend can forgive you for being unreachable. A girl that good-looking doesn't have to forgive shit, and she probably won't wait long when there is a line at her door of perfectly good suitors."

"Yeah, I just feel like she doesn't need me. She needs a dude who can be there more. I have way too much going on. I don't open up enough for her. I can't really be the guy she deserves." I froze.

I just said something out loud about my feelings. I don't do that. What the fuck was happening? I don't think he registered that this was new and weird to me, because he just kept talking.

"Well, either way, it would be cool if you two wanted to go out sometime. I know a double date is below you, but that is your first real girlfriend in a while, and I am so fucking sick of the couples that Amber wants to hang out with."

Normal married guy problems. For the first time ever, I wished I had the stasis that Jeremy did. I used to disdain that simplicity and predictability, but now, with a death under my belt and a slew of smaller problems, I had this small but growing desire for simplicity and predictability.

"Chase doesn't do anything like that, yet. It is a small matter of time, I guess. If I don't completely ruin things." I let out a nervous laugh. I don't think I ever did that before. That or the fucking talk about my relationships. Those are mine; I don't need help to do what I do. I help people. Not the other way around.

"Well, I recommend strongly that you be that dude who is more available. For her sake. And yours. I haven't seen you in a while either way, this would be a good chance to kill six birds with one stone. Make the girls happy, see each other and have a good meal, which I have not done in quite a while. Amber is on this cooking trip right now, but she is awful. I lie of course, but, Jesus. I need to eat some real food, and soon."

"Life sounds pretty bad, my friend. I will call soon. We can get that meal. We'll 'touch bases.'"

"Fuck you, T." He didn't like the reference.

"Bye, dude."

After we hung up I thought about his wisdom. He wasn't trying to give me advice, he just said what he said and it sounded so good. That is what I would do with my clients. They wanted to be more like me, so I just had to talk, and they listened. Now I wanted something more like Jeremy had and when he talked I listened like a goddamn client. Pathetic.

I sat there looking at the books on my shelf. I hadn't really read much since I started writing my own. I didn't want to dilute my insights with the ideas of other people. My ideas had to be completely outside of the box. Outside of the norm. Maybe that was why I had such a hard time getting publishers to see where I was coming from.

I looked at my manuscript. It sat alone on its own corner of my desk. Next to the computer that Chase helped me buy. I needed an outside of the box solution.

I had probably memorized the entire book. I was anal about editing it myself. I must have read it 50 times before I printed it. Not that 500 spelling and grammar mistakes didn't make it past my gaze, but I knew the concepts inside and out. When I read all those times, one thing was different: Me. Now I was a guy looking for something and I had a source of something.

Before I did anything, I was going to act. I thought Jeremy was on to something and I needed to muster up the gumption to be honest with a girl.

I picked my phone up again and thought about what I would say to her.

It never came. The words were not there. The sentiment

was not there. The only thing that I really had was a small sense of needing to win, and until I knew that telling her, or telling anyone the truth was a victory, I wasn't going to do it.

I guess it was a victory in some human sense. In some religious context, the truth is the be-all-end-all. But I was never religious, besides a short stint of Wednesday nights at the local Non-Denominational Church where three of the five hottest girls in high school went. I banged one of them and that ended my involvement with youth group.

I needed more than advice before I went around telling everyone 'the truth'.

Until then I had a book of my own to re-read and some thinking to do.

CHAPTER 24

The Open Book

A guy can be an open book, but his ability to 'close' is inversely proportional to how open he really is.

Lying is too complicated a tool for the hedonist, but a strict policy of keeping everything close to the vest is a sure fire way to stay in control of information. Information is what women use against you when weighing whether or not you are a suitable mate (ten-night stand).

Jealous girls require a certain amount of information, and I say, give them as much as it takes. Give them whatever convoluted half-truths they want to feed their voracious appetites, but never give them ammo. Always offer up sugar cubes of truth to stay in the game. If she wants depleted uranium shells for her arsenal, get the hell out of there. What you did last Friday night should always take about two sentences to answer, never more than that.

Honesty really is the best policy. But be careful what you are honest about.

Something occurred to me when I was eating a slice of pizza, looking at my manuscript. I was looking at it to reminisce about my moral flexibility in days of old. I looked at a stack of 160 pages, 1.5 spaced, size 14 font and wondered to myself what was so different about one year ago. Back then I don't think I would have lost a wink of sleep if I knew that someone fucked up because of what direction I steered him. Was I a bad person? Or was I blinded by my ego? I sat alone for two hours and glazed over my old lesson plans, wondering what changed inside of me, hoping to find some inspiration. Others found my guidance to be adequate. My survivors, at least. Maybe I could find something there.

Ultimately, I knew I couldn't take my own advice because it was bullshit. I guess the only thing to do was assume my moral compass pointed south and go the opposite direction.

Next to my manuscript was the notebook (one of many) that I was writing in the other night. I saw my note tucked in between two pages:

'Call Chase. Say Sorry.'

Ironic.

I had to tell Chase about the Laura thing. I had to do a lot of things but that was a good start. So much for taking the advice I laid out in my own book.

I knew it was a bad idea. It doesn't take a rocket scientist to figure out that this was going to very seriously complicate things, and I wasn't going to get the advantage back. In the push and pull of social networking, dating and sleeping around, this kind of honesty is suicide. I was about to owe a huge emotional debt to Chase but it didn't matter. I had to make a few things right at some point.

This was an all-new low for me.

I wanted to see her, I had my reasons to see her, but in all reality, I knew it wasn't going to be the same carefree fun that we had in the beginning. The first thing to go when this period of my life started was my sense of humor. That is what every girl on earth wants. Any guy who has ever read the interviews with Playmates, Penthouse Pets, and the Beauties of Hustler, Club and a million other smut mags knows that a sense of humor is high on every girl's list of qualities a guy must have. The main difference being that Playmates and Pets *date* funny guys, while girls in some of the other magazines are more interested in doing ass to mouth with those guys. It's all relative, but the bottom line is always humor. With Chase, it was more a matter of dating. We had our other forms of bonding, but I was the reason we weren't doing those. I figured she was losing interest. I'm right too often to shrug off my own theories, so it weighed on me that this was ending, along with the manslaughter, the pregnancy/Marines thing and how abysmal my failures actually felt. I almost felt pity for the people I helped.

Almost.

It was mostly self-pity, and in some twisted way a new form of pleasure that I had never experienced. In my years of being the center of my own universe, I was so shielded from the metaphorical miles of walking in other people's shoes, that in almost doing so recently I may have related to another person emotionally. At the end of the day, I have been so prone to doing things that felt good for me, that when I hit rock bottom, I wasn't dying to crawl out of it because I felt justified sleeping in on Saturdays and not talking to everyone, or answering my phone, or the million other pleasures of introversion. Those pleasures came at the sacrifice of the old pleasures. Those would come back in time. Right? I think that as long as people didn't know what was going on inside of me, I could still reach out and take anything that I wanted, the way that I used to. I just didn't want to.

I called her the next morning as a dry run. I didn't admit to myself that I knew she would be working and would not answer the phone.

What luck? She didn't answer. I did the next best thing and left an innocuous message about getting together sometime soon.

Within a few hours, right around her lunch break, I got the call back:

"I miss you, Chase."

"Hum, I miss you too." She didn't sound like the girl that I was fucking the hell out of a couple of weeks before. I didn't sound like the guy that was doing it to her necessarily, but I had my reasons.

"I want to see you soon. Can we talk about something?"

"Sure, T. How about we get together for coffee sometime soon. I will be at work until like six. Maybe seven tonight?"

"How about seven fifteen?" I needed this to be on my terms. Probably the last time things would be on my terms with her, if we even talked again.

"Okay, sure. Is everything alright? You haven't called in a few days."

"Yeah, I guess. I mean, some things are great; some things are really fucked up. I guess that's life, though."

"Mr. Life Coach. . .So wise." She laughed a little.

I felt a small wave of relief. If I could just tell her everything, maybe I would feel a complete relief. Maybe all of my problems would just go away.

As seven rolled around and I rolled up to the coffee shop we agreed to meet at via text, I saw her car. I always preferred to be the early one. I liked the image of someone walking in and greeting me. I don't like to be the one to walk in and go to someone else. It's just not me.

This was going to be on her terms, after all.

Well, maybe not.

I drove out of the parking lot and kept going. Seven fifteen is what we agreed on. Why would I lie and show up early?

I didn't have somewhere to go and I didn't have much time, so I drove around for about ten minutes and came back the exact opposite way another ten minutes. I had music on so I missed her two texts:

Where are you? (7:13)

Humm? (7:17)

In my defense, the music was a compilation of my favorite songs from artists that I don't normally tell people that I like. I wouldn't call myself a "Diamond Fan" *per se*, but I went through a phase where I knew all of the lyrics to "Sweet Caroline" and "Soolaimon". Both of which were on that album. Others that I included: "The Dance" by Garth Brooks, some Mamas and Papas and a Van Morrison song. I hate Van Morrison, but I like "Brown Eyed Girl".

I parked, walked in and saw her immediately. When I went over to sit, she asked if I wanted anything as she was getting up. I smiled and followed her to the counter. The barista was the engaged chick that I asked out the day I met Chase. I didn't know if that was a sign. I don't believe in those, but it was a valid question. My beliefs were reduced to shards over the last few weeks, so I dropped the habit of discounting things merely because I didn't believe in them.

My tea was hot and black. She got a Mocha. The coffee was going to keep her up all night. She would have been up all night if I went home with her. No, this time she is going to stay up all night tonight thinking about what a bastard I am.

"I'm worse than you thought."

I didn't know where my wording came from. What the fuck was I doing?

"I got someone killed, I'm failing out of school more or less and I have ruined a few other lives. I don't think I am good enough for you."

Wow. That just came out. Holy fuck. I felt way better. Mostly, that is, until I mustered up the strength to raise my eyes from the cup of tea in front of me and make eye contact with Chase. I didn't feel better after a few more seconds. Her confusion was better than the shock and hurt that I was expecting. Steeping the teabag was my nervous habit for the duration of this chat.

"Can you say that again? Just some of it. A little at a time."

I guess those are not things one anticipates talking about over coffee one random weeknight.

"I know this is a lot to take in. I don't date. I don't respect anyone. I don't open up. *Normally* I don't open up."

The words were just flowing. I don't really recall if I was articulate or fumbling. I was not a nervous talker. I was not a lot of things, but I became some of them at that moment.

"That buddy of mine that OD'ed, he was one of my clients. I introduced him to a new group of friends to get him out of his shell and they got him into coke. His mother somehow knew and blamed me."

"That is what all of this is about?"

"All of what?"

"The way you have been acting lately."

"Uh, yeah. I guess. I mean, yeah. It's been kind of shitty."

"Why didn't you tell me?"

I was beginning to like the Q&A format this was taking on. I didn't have to volunteer a lot of information if she kept asking specific questions.

"I don't normally talk about stuff like this with people. Not with you, not with anyone."

She sat quiet for a few seconds. It looked like she was thinking about what to say. I still didn't know if she was on my side, or the rest of the world's. . .

"You didn't sell it to him, you didn't make him do it. That was his choice, Tristan. You cannot hold it against yourself that someone else paid for decisions he made."

Her immediate response was positive. I thought for a moment that this could be alright.

"I tried telling myself that, Chase. But I just couldn't believe it."

"I wouldn't believe it if you said it either. You are too good at making complete BS sound so good."

"Well, I guess it is easier to believe coming from you, maybe I am not that horrible after all."

"Okay, see, T.? You can open up to me. It's not going to kill you to connect with another person outside of the bedroom."

It was true. I started to feel way better, and I wondered if I should have just been honest with her the whole time. I guess so, huh? I could see it in her eyes that she cared about me and wanted this to work out. I always knew that people cared about me, but I didn't let it affect me. This time it was something completely different.

I know my limits. I don't have many of them, but I do know exactly how far ahead I was and in the three seconds it took her to tell me that everything was okay I made the decision never to utter Laura's name again.

"I know this sucks, and I have never had baggage until just after we met, but do you think we could still see each other?"

I know I sounded like a pussy, but I liked how this was panning out. I wanted more.

"Of course, Tristan. Why wouldn't we. Unless you go to prison, that is. . ."

I stared at her. Speechless.

"Too soon?" she asked. She added on, "Are you giving up your life coaching thing?"

"I think. I guess, I mean it's probably not the best time."

"Good. I didn't like it. I think you are smart, Tristan, but I don't think you are really acting in anyone's interest when you do that stuff."

I didn't know whether to be offended or to just be glad that we had come to this point. So I shrugged it off and we finished our drinks together.

CHAPTER 25

The Importance of the Process

There are 99 ways to skin a cat. But there are most likely just one or two that suit each person best. The idea behind consistently making progress towards one's goals is that the right process will yield results every time, and little by little, you can chisel away at obstacles and rough edges until you have created your own statue of David.

Academic probation sucks. I have seen it done, first hand, and heard of different methods from friends in other schools. Mine was relatively light, and I just had to meet with a counselor every week and give her a head's up about my attendance and my involvement and all the other bullshit that I didn't want her to micromanage. The problem was that *my* counselor was out of town for about a month—as of last week. I had to meet with a large and ineffectual substitute career counselor, who did this job because she probably couldn't have succeeded anywhere else in life. I didn't mind it at first, but after about ten seconds of being patronized about how smart I was and how I was not living up to my potential, I had had enough.

"You are so smart, Tristan. You really could go far if you think about your potential."

Complete bullshit.

I sat there, thinking about how she could really use a few lessons from me about how to talk people into things. She took a cookie-cutter leadership approach—assuming that I was going to take what she said to heart because she was in a position of 'authority' over me.

I reciprocated in the most acquiescing tone I could muster:

"I know. I know. I try to imagine my goals and then come up with a path to them." I was paraphrasing a poster on her wall. "But I guess I am not that smart after all, because it always gets blurry. It's like there is no real path to what I want." I gave her the opportunity of a lifetime to give me the most contrived guidance she could make up off the top of her head.

"Tristan, you need to bring them into focus. You need perspective, you need measurable goals and you need to know the results you expect to get from your efforts."

Yep. The goal was to let her take the requisite amount of time she needed to 'guide' me, the perspective was looking up at her genius, and the results were that she could feel like we made a breakthrough.

It honestly sounded like she was reading this from a script. I didn't like her much already. But after that exchange, I decided that I was going to push a bookshelf on top of her and walk out.

"What are your goals, Tristan?"

To sleep with 1,000 (quality) girls; To write books for the men of the 21st century; To have more money than I can spend; And to get my way, every time, no matter what.

"I guess I want to get by in school, and eventually get a good job." I want this session to fucking end.

"You have all of the tools you need to do that right here, you know that?"

The tools that were available to me were the scissors on her desk, or the letter opener that was probably in her desk drawer. There was an artery somewhere under the roughly 36% body fat. There were also an unlimited number of blunt objects at my disposal. If I could figure out a way to make her hear herself talk, maybe that would kill her. I think, however, that the deadliest tool in her office was the advice that I came up with myself. I tried to sound curious and into her advice, but not so curious that she would talk much more.

"Really? I guess I never thought about the resources we have here. I always just try to go about it alone."

I could have achieved any nuance I wanted and she still would not have picked up on shit. She heard what she thought were pleas for help and then she heard the garbage that she spewed as real guidance. I don't have to wonder too much when I am ever posed with questions about the future of our country. I just look at the people trying to shape the young minds.

Also, on that note, I would say that we are completely fucked, based on my limited experience in the institutions that shape the minds of tomorrow.

"There are plenty of old fossils like me who have been around the block and can give all sorts of advice." She laughed at her own joke. I felt bad that she thought her advice was valid, but then again, I didn't have much of a leg to stand on. Mine sure as hell wasn't.

I looked at my watch. "Class soon, I would hate to be late."

She nodded in understanding. She could now justify another paycheck for another two weeks based solely on our little chat today.

All in all, things were going well academically. I was still in a tight spot and had another month of being careful before finals this semester, but I could probably breathe a little more easily if I just pulled this off now.

There was a little more to the conversation, nothing worth recalling, so long as I made it implicitly clear what kind of moron I was up against. With that I walked out of her office and shut the door behind me. I leaned against it to be dramatic and let out a deep breath. I could see a few other women in the office laugh to themselves that another person had to listen to the wisdom of Miss. . .I looked at the nameplate on the door: Mrs. Daily.

She was married? Poor bastard.

As I gladly left that place, I began to think about what my actual goals were. Hmmm.

The thing about the 1,000 girls was true, so was all the other stuff, but there are usually about seven million steps in the middle that keep people from their goals. I was somewhere on step 11. I guess at this point I just needed to figure out where to go from there.

It occurred to me that between smoothing things over with Chase, and finally getting to the point where I wouldn't have to sweat school much longer, that things were kind of turning around. Things had been okay as far as school went for about two weeks, so I guess I mostly owed my relief to the little talk with Chase the other day. We had plans to go out with Jeremy and Amber the coming weekend and a couple of free nights between then to see each other more. I owed it to myself to get out of this rut. I hadn't had sex in a couple of weeks, and I can't remember the last time I laughed out of pleasure. I laughed on the inside while I was talking to Mrs. Daily, but I also got a little sad inside that she was so deluded.

I walked out of that office, pockets stuffed with brochures for "job opportunities" and half a mind to take a look at some of the things that the average Joes here were going to resign themselves to. I guess it was a possibility that I would have to get a real job at some point. I didn't plan on doing it for long, but every good dive needs a springboard, and sometimes you have to work with what you've got. In my assessment of the worst-case scenario, I would have to get a real job while I worked out my master plan. So, this was essentially my worst-case scenario. I told myself that since I still had a few ideas, I was not completely fucked, but I was on the cusp.

When I walked out of the building, I began a long jaunt around the campus. I hadn't looked at any of the brochures and didn't really think that any of them applied to my major, but it was a back-step in the right direction. I think. I guess that is at least what everyone else thinks.

Insurance for squandered dreams.

CHAPTER 26

In another book, in another format, this would be called 'Part II', or possibly 'Part Two'. As a new chapter unfolds in one's life and one has already used the chapter concept to isolate anecdotes, the only logical way to break it up is with 'Parts'. I don't want to do that because this isn't an epoch, and my life has not been long enough to have a 'Part II', yet. As my emotional journey through adolescence goes, this is roughly 'Part 16'. I prefer roman numerals (Roman Numerals? roman numerals? I don't know): 'Part XVI'. At least I know how to write them.

Chase was freaking out. She hadn't been acting the same as the smoking hot chick that I met five weeks prior. Given the shit that I went through and did, I guess I couldn't really hold it against her and I tried not to hold grudges or repress anything. I think she was just acting like more of a girlfriend and that was to be expected. The 'issue' (I think it warrants these things: '') is that she was acting like a girl. I didn't care about the girlfriend part. I didn't really long-term-date up to this point, so I was not used to waiting on a girl, or trying to appease her at any level deeper than saying what I needed to say to sleep with her. That never really involved having the same conversation with her over and over about how she looks in a certain outfit. Of course, I had the same conversation with about 70 of them. But it wasn't the same chick 70 times. That is totally different and FUCKING ANNOYING. Oh well.

"I don't like these pants." She was dead set on making us

late to dinner with Jeremy and Amber. I wasn't thrilled about a double date and I wasn't dying to go by any measure, but I was ready and didn't want to wait around for her to try on four outfits that looked the same to me.

"No way. I think they look great."

C'mon, look convincing. . .

"I think I gained a few pounds."

This has to be a trap.

"Is this a trap?"

She didn't think it was funny. In spite of the light I tried to make of it, I think the gain of a few pounds is also not funny. Every chick out there that is the size of a school bus or a small earthmover was thin once. Maybe at the age of two, or maybe as late as her twenties. But really, it started with a few pounds and then after hearing "No, you look fine" roughly 20 times, she is a few multiplied by 20 pounds heavier. That is 60 LBS. Not okay. Not remotely okay.

"Babe, you look fine." She gets two freebies and then we have a talk.

"You're just saying that."

"Would I take you into public if I didn't approve?" I just realized that I sound like a total asshole. Obviously my inner monologue is pretty blunt, but every one's is. I wanted to be as good a boyfriend as I was a womanizer. And from the sound of things, I was not quite there. Yet.

Fortunately, she laughed at my joke and we left. Almost on time. Almost.

I want to just keep writing that the car ride was uneventful, but we had a milestone together.

"I'm really glad that you quit Life Coaching, Tristan. I think you would be great at it. But I also think that you should do some classes or something, you know? Do they have those?"

I was driving, so I just gripped the steering wheel harder until my knuckles were white and kept staring at the road.

"Yeah. I don't like the courses. They teach everyone the same shit that the counselors at school teach."

"Don't you think that's good? They are counselors for a reason."

"Yeah, if they wanted people to excel they might have better advice than the bullshit motivational posters all over their walls." I was speaking from experience.

"Well, speaking from experience, I would say I had a pretty good counselor."

"How?" The gloves were coming off.

"She got me set up as an intern where I work now. I get paid pretty well, I would say. She also talked me through a bad breakup I had my freshman year."

Mental note: find out about this boyfriend.

"So she helped you enter the workforce and keep the gears of society turning at the expense of your talent."

I know how I meant it, but I was hoping to god that she heard it the same way.

"So I am just a keg in a wheel to you?"

Nope. I say talent and she hears expendable. This was not covered in Psych 301.

"It's a cog, not a keg. Or peg? Whatever." I couldn't see her eyes because I was 'focusing' on the road, but I could tell that pissed her off. "The point is that you are awesome and she thought that you should limit yourself to some part-time job when you could do anything you want."

Good save. I think.

"It's a full time job, Tristan."

There was silence for about 30 seconds. I think it felt like longer, but I still let that kind of shit roll off, so I kept driving, focusing on the road and humming to myself.

"And you know what else, Tristan?"

This was going to be good.

"What, Babe?"

"I may be a peg or whatever you said, but at least I have a job. You don't even contribute."

I would say that it hurt, but I can't even pretend that it bothered me. I don't pay taxes that I don't believe in. I don't have a boss that I hate. I don't have to spend my free time making someone else rich while I slave away for 8, 9 or 10 dollars an hour. Besides not having a house that I cannot afford and a shit load of debt, I am living the American dream.

"You're right."

I did need a new source of income, though. She was right about that. If she even said that. I don't think she did. But she got me thinking about it.

That just about ended everything. But I had to go for a Hail Mary. There was one more thing I needed to gauge.

"Are you on your period, Chase?"

"Yes."

Now I know.

"Why?"

"Because I wanted to know if you would like to get some chocolate ice cream after we eat with Jeremy and Amber."

I'm a doll. I know.

"You're a doll, Tristan."

I know.

When we arrived at Andolinni's (I think I spelled it correctly), Jeremy and Amber were already there. It was an okay Italian place. I don't love Italian, so I was going to get the least messy thing I could find on the menu and pick at it for the duration of the meal. Unfortunately for me and my propinquity for not getting covered in marinara, I could not find a single goddamn thing on the menu that fit the bill. Eggplant Parmesan would have to suffice. Also a red wine the waiter recommended and a side of bowtie pasta with a veggie medley. Chase went with some salad *al diavola*. It had those delicious shrimp in it. Good call on the salad, babe.

Chase was normally super charming around people. Especially when we first met, but tonight her game was slightly off. She wasn't that engaged with my friend. Friends, I guess, if I were counting Amber. And this time I would. She was accommodating for my date being the quiet buzzkill. She had to excuse herself about four times during the meal, each time prompting,

"Is she okay?" from one or the other.

Jeremy laughed at me when I rolled my eyes at her third and fourth exit from the conversation.

"How is it being in a normal relationship?"

"You call that normal behavior?"

"T., for being so smart about people, you don't have the slightest clue about what a normal relationship is, do you?"

"Apparently not."

Amber piped in "That's normal. She's probably just on her cycle. I'll go talk to her."

"Thanks, Amber." Amber, the biological savant. How the hell did she know? That was amazing. I guess I did have a lot to learn about this stuff.

After she got up as well, Jeremy leaned in, looked over his shoulder to ensure the ball and chain was far enough away, and said "Dude, she is smoking. I don't care if she was the wicked witch of the west. You got yourself quite a trophy."

"I liked her for other reasons too."

"Sure, man. Sure." He was not completely convinced, and he had no reason to be. She had not said ten words or really smiled all night.

We both sat back and took a sip of our wine. We didn't need to talk. This was the first time all night that there wasn't some forced conversation about shit we don't normally talk about unless girls are around. We would usually just talk about them. But I guess it is not polite to discuss how to effectively do the jackhammer to Amber when she is sitting right there eating Pasta Primavera. She may not have approved. That was one of the last conversations we had. That and the Gay-Date. Maybe I should bring that up. . .

"Look, T. Over there." He motioned towards the back end of the restaurant. There stood the best-looking waitress I had ever seen. She looked more like a super model wearing the stupid ass white, button-down shirt with frills.

"Wow." I was at a loss for words. I would have normally already thought of something to say and been half way to her.

But this relationshippy stuff made me prostrate. I could not only not think of something to say, I was not allowed to say it.

And then, just past her came our two girls. They were still the best-looking girls in the joint, and probably even the whole city, but waitress was something else. She had black hair and cat-like features; high cheek bones, dark eyes and an exotic curvaceous body that no guy deserves. I smiled at Chase who gave me a similar look. Jeremy did the same thing to his date. We were guilty as sin of staring at her, but we could play it off.

They sat down and both just stared at us. Chase looked over at the waitress and back at me. She was less than pleased.

"Who's hungry?" I tried to act more excited about my eggplant and dug in.

Without being able to really predict the future, I knew my assessment for the rest of the night was probably going to be pretty close: Rain with a chance of thunder.

CHAPTER 27

Chance

Everything is a numbers game. The more you say yes the more doors you open. Any idiot knows this, but few live it. There are a million traps you may lay ahead of yourself in doing so, but an adept eye should have no problem seeing these.

Few shitty things are actually blessings in disguise, but those come along too. When talking to guys about it, one should address the situation as 'completely from one's own doing', as he is the master of his own destiny. When seducing women, employ the word 'serendipitous'. Happy guys that always get laid know how to take the right angle based on their audiences.

The dinner with Jeremy and Amber was not a smashing success, but it did teach me about the way things are now. After we got home that night, we didn't really fight or argue. She just pent everything up and went to bed without saying a lot. I used my schoolwork as an excuse to go home and left. We didn't even go to ice cream afterwards.

I had learned that I cannot look or touch. I knew I couldn't touch, but I didn't know that committed girlfriends were so touchy about merely glancing over and seeing who another girl was. In spite of how shitty the whole thing was and how it was entirely her fault, Jeremy and I were grateful that we conditioned the girls to think that double dates were crap. Also, I still really liked her. I wanted to do something to make things right before she went to bed, but I didn't really know how. Everything was different. I was a maser when it came to girls I didn't know, but this was beyond me. It's like the girlfriend rulebook was written in Arabic.

I woke up the next morning to a phone call. At first, I thought it was one of the guys I used to help. I kind of hoped it was. I wanted to do something. I needed to feel like I was really good at something. I was always good at everything I did. But I spent too long marginalizing the meaning of school, so much so that since I had brought my grades back up it didn't feel like I had done anything except make a bunch of other people happy. Namely my fucking counselor, who was not even a real counselor. I didn't consider her a real person, nonetheless a legitimate counselor. I didn't even care what my real counselor thought, so when I made the idiot happy, I felt like I was doing humanity a disservice by showing her that her help was effective.

"Hello?" I tried not to sound groggy.

"Tristan? Did I wake you?"

You are adept, my friend. Now who the fuck are you?

"No, I'm good. Who is this?"

"This is Professor Sandoval. I'm the director of the History department."

"Oh, okay. What can I do for you?" I think I knew who he was.

"I was talking to some of the counselors looking for someone to tie up some odds and ends a few hours a week, and Mrs. Daily said that she knew of a very competent young man who was looking for something."

"I would have thought you had a line of people willing to do that stuff for you."

"There is a very long line, but I really just wanted someone who didn't want to earn brownie points and could do simple taskings without trying to get me to call Princeton and put in a good word."

He seemed down to earth. I really hated that Mrs. Daily animal for throwing me under the bus, but I did need a new source of income. Eventually my well would dry up. The shit that I would make working for him would likely just slow down the drying of my well.

"When do I start?"

"Why don't you come in today around three and we will talk."

"Sounds good. I'll see you at three."

I make it a point not to say 'Sir' when I talk to those guys. I don't think they do anything to distinguish themselves. They just stayed in a job long enough to work their way up. The fact that they did it for an institution that is almost as old as society does not make it special. It's just a job. Most of them didn't like that about me. I hoped Sandoval didn't care.

"See you at three, Tristan."

Even though I changed some pretty significant aspects of my life, the number of dates and times I set didn't seem to diminish in the slightest.

It made me kind of nostalgic about the days where I would have 13 places to be. It was like solving a puzzle, trying to figure out when and where I would have to be.

I wondered what the hell I was going to do for this guy. Hopefully I would not have to grade essays. I hated reading what other people my age wrote. They didn't write what needed to be said, they wrote what they thought some professor (or TA, in most cases) wanted to hear.

As three drew closer, I started to get ready. I assumed I already had the 'job', so I didn't feel like I had to dress like I was going to an interview. And given Sandoval's disparaging opinion of TAs trying to suck him off, I figured casual would be right up his alley.

I walked down the wing of the History building that his office was likely to be in. I was also correct in assuming so, because he had the biggest office I had ever seen. Not that I had been in copious offices on this campus, but the dude had quite a place. He was at his desk and the door was open, so I walked in and introduced myself.

"Good morning, Professor."

I took a look around before sitting. He had some relics and a few busts of god-knows-who.

"Do you see that over there?" He pointed towards a book that had it's own case. "That is a 400-year-old Bible."

"Wow." I was not impressed because I didn't care much for that kind of stuff, and the words in every Bible were all the same age. Also, I don't know Latin, so it was unreadable as far as I was concerned.

"I like you, Tristan. I like your demeanor."

He got my attention.

"How do you mean?"

"People who want to work for me pretend to be more interested in this stuff than they are. I don't see one inkling of that from you."

I grinned. I couldn't think of a response to him telling me that it was obvious that I didn't care about his book.

"Anyhow," he went on "I have to teach a course for someone who will not be finishing out the semester and there is no way I am going to grade all of those papers myself."

Son of a bitch! I knew it. Grading papers.

"I can imagine."

"You aren't going to afford a BMW doing this, but I worked it out with the school and I have added this position as an assistant job, so you will make about a hundred bucks a week. It will at least pay for gas and beer. I don't know what else your generation is into."

"I'm saving up my money to buy a book like that."

He laughed. "I'll bet you are, Tristan. What do you say you come in on Thursday and pick up the first stack of essays? They are short. I don't even know what they are on yet. We can talk about the grading criteria and then you will have all weekend to take care of them. Sounds good?"

Sounds miserable.

"Yeah, sounds great."

He shook my hand and I walked out to my car, which

was half the campus away. I needed to see Chase. She was at work, so I stopped and got her a half-quart of Ben and Jerry's. When I went in she was actually happy to see me. I didn't know if there were going to be repercussions for last night, but I quit worrying about those instantly.

She gave me a big hug. I could tell that the two nerds in there with her hated my guts for being the guy that she was with. As if they had a chance with a girl like her. I got a small laugh from their burning stares.

"Tristan, have you met the guys?"

"Hum, I can't say that I have." I was getting more pleasure by the second.

"This is. . ."

I don't recall their names, because they were inconsequential dudes, but shaking their hands and smiling, and introducing myself as Chase's boyfriend was the highlight of my day. Especially considering I just pigeonholed myself into grading fucking essays this weekend.

And that was it. She was okay. I had a 'job'. Everything was copacetic.

I think.

CHAPTER 28

The Autodidact

The self-educated man, even one with the magical piece of paper from a university, knows how to learn from anything. He knows that education and lessons are available everywhere and he knows that there is not enough time to perfect each life lesson by doing things the hard way. Don't waste too much time looking for instructions. Don't go out of your way for cheap lessons when so many seek you out on their own.

The weather had improved and I was finally at a stable place. I had just picked up the stack of papers from Sandoval and Chase's cycle was back to a place where we could do more than kiss without ruining her white sheets. I guess this was what I had needed for the last two months, this stability.

I arranged a lunch with Jeremy to discuss the damage from our gawking and just get away from those goddamned papers that I had not even looked at yet. I didn't know if Amber was as easily appeased as Chase, but I had a feeling that if they were discussing marriage then she was going to be a total bitch about it. That is just where those relationships usually stand. When the time came, I got into my car, rolled the windows down and put on NPR.

I don't like NPR. I don't normally follow the news. I hadn't just begun to care, but a former client emailed me that there was going to be something of interest on and that I should give it a listen. And so I did.

It was an interview with a dude who became a pretty prominent Life Coach. He was talking about society's need for what he called Wellness Coaches.

> "(. . .) The 40-hour workweek, the rigidity of television scheduling, the negative, fear driven news: All of these are things that just take joy from people. The list goes on. They not only take joy, they take the time that someone could use to make his or her life better. They put this negative pressure on everyone. What I do, through exercise programs, meditation practices and various activities, is try to relieve some of that pressure."

The guy was really articulate, and it sounded like he had said this piece about a million times, but I liked it. It reminded me of the days of old. Like a few months ago.

I didn't catch the whole thing, but I got what I needed from it. A dose of nostalgia. Those things that the guy was talking about, the average person's life, were things that my life was shaping into more and more by the day. Maybe I should have written his name down and given him a call in a few years when I finally completed my transformation into a completely average asshole. I already needed the wellness.

Maybe he had openings for jobs. I was obviously a good fit. I had a little bit of on-the-job experience and I knew all about amelioration. I found mine. I guess. I drove a little slower so that I could hear more of the interview and some of this guy's outlook. I think it was predictable and cookie-cutter, but he was right. There are so many people out there who waste themselves, their time, their lives, their families, sitting in front of a television. I felt kind of inspired, but inspired to what? That was the question.

I pulled up to that Cuban place Jeremy and I usually ate at. I saw his car already there but I waited for a minute longer to hear a little more of this interview. I wasn't getting anything out of it at this point, but I was getting something out of listening just to listen. I could see Jeremy in the window of the restaurant ordering something. Maybe he would get me a tea.

I picked up my phone and sent him a text: Order me an iced tea.

He looked out of the window and saw me. I waved and he flipped me off. Good friend.

When I walked inside the waitress brought me a tea. Good friend.

I didn't have much going on, which was not normal for me, but had recently become pretty commonplace. So I let him kick off.

"How is your girl?"

"She's fine." I responded. "How's yours?"

"She didn't say anything about that chick at Andolinni's." (I think I spelled it right.)

"Well, I always had a rule: There is ONE girl who would not count as cheating, and if I ever got a chance I would let her have it."

"Everyone has that rule, Tristan. Amber's is, fuck, I don't remember his name. One of those fag singers."

"I know, huh. They are all so gay with their millions of dollars and the ability to have almost any girl they want. So gay. . ."

"Mine is that one model from those Doritos commercials."

"I know who she is." And she was hot. I had to give him kudos for his taste in the women that he will never have.

"What about you?"

"I don't pick mine until the last minute."

"What do you mean?"

"I don't pick someone I will never meet. I leave it open and if I get a chance to sleep with a beautiful girl I choose her. Then it is not cheating."

"You can't do that, dude."

"Well, I never really had a 'girlfriend' (I did air quotes)

like this, so I don't really have such a base rule now, but before, if I was kind of exclusive, I would use that rule religiously."

"You are one fucked up dude."

"I get by." I thought for a second. "I don't do shit like that anymore, but I guess, if I had to pick, for normalcy's sake, I would definitely choose that waitress."

"And that wouldn't be cheating?"

"No, everyone has that rule, right?"

"Yeah, but I think it only works if you both tell each other."

"Okay, fuck, that is not going to happen. I wasn't even allowed to look over at that chick. I think her name is forbidden, if I even knew it."

"Yeah, no shit. I don't think we are allowed to know it. . ." He looked guilty of something.

"What do you know that I don't?"

"It's Sara." He finally gave in. "I saw her name as we were leaving. It was an accident. I was trying to look at her tits without Amber noticing."

"Maybe I *am* a better boyfriend than you."

"I doubt that."

I think his doubts were well founded. But I was trying. That has to count for something. And then, just because someone mentioned being a good boyfriend, she walked by. She was that hot little number that I used to try to come here hoping to sleep with. I cursed Jeremy for not choosing to sit in her section.

"Well, either way you look at it, I wasn't the one *looking at her name*."

We both laughed. I ended up eating one of their world famous (in my mind) empanadas and chatted about nothing in particular with Jeremy. I got scared when he talked about getting married. I didn't think that it was something he should do until after they had both been out in the real world for a while. I used to get scared that he wouldn't sleep with more women, but by then my worldview was changing one minute at a time.

That smoking little Cubana walked by our table to ask if

we wanted something more to drink, and I got nostalgic again for the days when I used to get any girl I wanted. But instead of letting that bother me, I just got a refill on my tea and started talking about Chase. Jeremy sensed something, because instead of listening, he just sat there grinning at me. He saw through my bullshit. I must have *really* lost it, because I couldn't even bull-shit something that I thought was true. I really was happy that I had her. She got me through what must have been the most rough couple of months of my life. I'm not saying we should run off and elope, but she was pretty fucking badass for being there for me. A guy is allowed to be nostalgic, right?

I guess not. It isn't masculine. It makes me into a bad liar, and it is completely contrary to some of the only valid advice I used to give clients: don't fucking worry about yesterday. Keep moving. I never said it any other way. Everyone who ever paid me to make him cooler heard those exact words. Once, I even reformed someone who played D&D.

When she brought my tea back, it was a sweet tea. Not to complain, but I hate sweet tea. Maybe I built her up too much.

CHAPTER 29

Tristan,

First of all, I laughed my ass off when I read your email. You showed a certain amount of gumption that we don't ever see from writers. It became apparent to me that you really practice what you preach. I have spent the last couple of weeks making a pretty good case for you to my boss, and I think with a few (a lot of) tweaks, we could make your book into something printable. I don't want to get your hopes up too much, but it looks like we can make something happen. Contact me if you are interested or if you have any questions.

Joshua Diggins.

I really didn't remember exactly what he was talking about until I looked in my SENT MAIL folder. I also laughed my ass off and wondered to myself if that is what it would have taken in the first place.

I was also pretty torn up over the fact that he fucking wrote me back after I decided to forsake my practice. Can I call it that? I just like the sound of it. I guess I can. *The Devil's Advocate*; my practice. It sounded legalistic. Since it was non-existent, I could have called it anything I wanted. I guess I could still publish the book and just not coach anymore. That didn't make a ton of sense. Book tours would be kind of weird if I turned out to be the normal Joe that I was acting like now. While I was pretty conflicted over the whole thing I was pretty happy that my work was publishable. That is a feeling I have never had. It was more edifying than hitting the 100 mark (100 *quality girls* mark). It felt like the first time I got paid by a nerd to help him become more like me. It felt goddamn good.

I looked at my other emails. About once every couple of weeks I hear from someone new who got my email address from a former client or from a former client himself asking if I have time for a buddy of theirs. Needless to say, this was another one of those days where I got one of those emails. It was a guy named Shane. He was pretty hard up. I could tell by his writing. The worse off people are, the more they try to downplay it and write to me like they are trying to conduct some business trans-action. Not that it isn't, but the more someone tries to make it out to be *just* a business transaction, the more they need it. That is something that I learned pretty early on. I don't even respond to these guys anymore. It sucks too much turning them down because I am not going to lie and say I am too busy with other people, and I cannot bring myself to say that I don't do it any-more.

What I am too busy for is to have this job working for Sandoval. There were more papers than I thought and as I said, I passionately hate the way people my age write. There is no excuse for being so stupid when one pays so much money for an education. There is also no excuse for not properly citing sources and not properly using footnotes. By the tenth paper, I become aware that I was also guilty as sin of numerous comma splices in my own book. There is just no need for them. If I didn't gouge my eyes out from grading these papers I should probably re-re-re-edit my book. God forbid I decide to go through with publishing.

Wait. Why the fuck wouldn't I publish? This was some-thing that I spent two years thinking about, I spent hours and hours of my life and my sanity trying to publish and now I sat at a desk with a stack of papers I didn't want to fucking read con-templating not fulfilling one of my dreams. Why would someone want a source of income from something he loved when he could very easily sell his soul and have a job he hated? Who wants to be his own boss anyhow?

I had no idea where these bullshit defeatist ideas were coming from.

I needed to quit thinking about it. I figured I would absolutely publish, but I really needed to finish off the papers at hand. The stack was still the size of a scale model of the Eiffel Tower and I had to finish them soon, at the risk of killing my weekend reading about whatever the hell these things were on. I would have like to reiterate it here, but now when I try to recall anything about them I still think of suicide.

After a couple of hours and thrice renouncing the education system, I took a break. I couldn't do it anymore. I especially couldn't do more and not be vindictive towards the poor idiots who happened to have papers at the bottom of the stack and not the top. I think I was getting more spiteful in my grading as the night wore on.

I called Chase. I got a hold of her and she was free for the night. So I stepped back to see the damage that I had inflicted on the pile of evidence that most people should not be allowed to breed. Or even breathe. I was satisfied with my progress and took a shower before heading over to her place.

I don't sing in the shower. I never did. When I think about it, I'll bet most people don't. But what I do do is have imaginary debates or arguments about whatever has pissed me off recently. I also used to rehearse the material I would use on clients. I never knew why, but I think being in the shower is a good way to clear my head. Or rather process the information that I fill it with. Tonight it was my case for publishing. I think I needed some convincing. And I was really the only man for the job.

I went to Chase's at about 7pm. I planned on spending the night, but I forgot my toothbrush so I spent the first five minutes of the ride contemplating turning around, stopping and buying a new one, or using hers without her knowing about it. The only reason for all of the deception was that she always freaked out about me using her toothbrush. She thought it was gross to begin with, but apparently there is some virus or disease one can get from toothbrush sharing. I didn't make a decision because it was something I could put off, but along the way I saw a drugstore and without even hitting my breaks I did a 45 mile an hour turn into the parking lot.

Bad move.

There was a cop sitting two spaces away from my parking spot. I mumbled something like 'fuck', but it may have been 'motherfucker'. He was one of those douche cops who didn't show any emotion. He walked up to my window and I handed him my license. He didn't say anything except, "Registration."

It was an order. Usually there was a please somewhere in there. Not this time. I handed it to him and waited while he sat in his car. I think he was actually jerking off to the power he had over me. I listened to music while I waited and tried not to let this get me down. I have had about three seatbelt tickets since I started driving, but no moving violations.

I could see him sitting there doing nothing. We were essentially parked next to each other so I could look over and watch him do jack shit while my girlfriend waited for me. My weekend was ticking by and since I wasn't getting paid by the hour like he was it became excruciating by the minute. I was getting really pissed off, but I just kept listening to my music and trying not to show it. The last thing I needed was for this prick to think that he needed to teach me a lesson.

And then finally he got out of his car. I smiled, but I was thinking something more along the lines of 'fuck you pig.' He swaggered over like a giant dick and handed me my papers, once again without showing any emotion.

"Slow it down a bit, okay?"

And he swaggered back over to his car and drove off.

"Wow." I sat there thinking about how wrong I was. That was amazing. It took about fifteen seconds for me to get my bearings back, I was still really confused, but I put my car in reverse and slowly backed out. I cautiously got back on the road and used my turn signals properly. I did everything by the book all the way to Chase's apartment.

"Babe, you won't believe what happened." I walked in as she was opening the door.

"What?" she asked.

"I just got out of a big-ass ticket, that's what."

"What where you doing?"

"Speeding, but I also had a kidnap victim in my trunk, and I was strung out on drugs."

"Oh, yeah, that is a pretty big ticket. What did you have to do to get out of it?"

"I can't tell you."

"Then should I sleep with you tonight?"

"Well, if I don't tell you what I had to do with that cop, then you have no reason to doubt my faithfulness."

"Great."

"Yeah, great."

We joked around and had a nice time. Nice time in terms of relationshippy stuff. We watched a movie and ate ice cream. I wondered what Jeremy and Amber did when they spent evenings together like this. I guess I knew all of the interesting stuff (like the jackhammer episode), but he never told me about the bullshit chick flicks that he was subjected to.

I don't remember the film we watched. I think I dozed off the entire time, but as it was winding to a close, Chase straddled me to wake me up. We kissed but had to move to the bedroom so she could show me a few moves that she read about in *Cosmo*. I was familiar, but didn't say so. Also, one of them threw me for a loop because to do the mermaid she needs to be on something higher than a bed. We made due and after about 90 minutes of exchanging heat, fluids and affections we both laid on our backs, quietly breathing and cooling off.

I suddenly realized that I never bought a toothbrush at the drugstore.

"Damn."

"What is it, T.?"
"Nothing, Babe."
I was just going to use hers tonight.

CHAPTER 30

The Well-Kept Secret

No matter what, do not dwell. Make the decision and stick with it. Be open or keep it close to the vest. Dwelling will cause things to come out subconsciously. When someone doesn't know you have a secret she will not look. When you beat around the bush, act differently, or allude surreptitiously to something that doesn't eventually come out, she will go looking.

When you consider something at length and then suppress it your vocabulary and your mannerisms will set you up for failure. You will talk about parallels and about whatever is in your head without knowing that you are betraying yourself. The man with a short memory for things that should not be brought up is the man without secrets.

There was no reason not to tell her that I was going to publish my book. What was weird is that I was hesitant in the first place. It was weird that I had to keep something so awesome a secret, but I didn't know if I actually did need to keep it a secret, or if I thought I had to. I didn't plan on telling her anything because I knew her stance on it.

It was Friday, which was a light enough day, and I figured I had enough time to knock out all of the grading I had to do and manage some schoolwork, which was getting exponentially lighter for me now that I had completely caught up in all of my classes. I had to meet Mrs. Whatever-the-fuck-her-name-was around lunch about my academic probation and then I was free to do whatever I wanted.

That was the exact moment in time that I will never forget. It was like reading the email from Ash's mom. Except it was I who was dead.

I had no idea what I wanted to do with my free time. I had no agenda. I had no purpose. I had no 'my thing'. I was going to hang out with Chase. Obviously. I had to make numerous tweaks to my book, but I didn't even know what those were, so I really just had to write an email back to Josh and tell him I was still interested. Maybe. I didn't even know if that was an avenue I was going to go down with my life. I was fucking 22, capable of anything and at a complete loss for what to do with Friday, Saturday and Sunday.

This realization seems anti-climactic. I just spent 2 months roaming around, doing schoolwork and wallowing over someone else's decisions. Why then would a couple of lazy days, unplanned days, regular weekend days be so bad to me? Here is exactly why:

I renounced this type of life for years. There was always some contribution to make to the master plan. There was always a way to make the master plan work. It was not a habit, it was the same clockwork that made me blink and breathe. It was my religion. My ethics came from the same thing that I no longer had. My master plan, my God, didn't have a shape. He was dead, and I had nothing but the shadow he cast as a remnant. I had nothing to get on track, to fix, to strive for. School was still a joke. If not just still, then more so after grading so many History papers. My work itself, Sandoval's job for me, was a nightmare, but I actually calculated it into my weekend plans, and thought they didn't exist, they were contingent on having free time from the essays. My relationship was good, but it was the same one for a while now. Nothing was there for me to make better.

Not even me. I didn't even have a way to make me better, and even though my life was pretty fucked up I got to be the driving force in fixing it.

As I thought about this I got physically worked up. I was taking deep breaths and not exhaling until I finished thoughts. I could feel my pulse rise ever so slightly. Like I said. This was groundbreaking for me. This was a moment that I was not going to forget.

My mood changed. I needed something. I looked at the papers. I gave a serious thought to telling Sandoval that I was done. I also gave serious thought to finishing them at that moment. When I understood that I was putting his needs before mine I walked out of my place to ensure that things happened in the correct order according to my nature. What I wanted to do is *numero uno*. What others expect from me comes second.

I took my laptop to a coffee shop to write Josh Diggins back. I was going to completely accept his offer to 'make something happen' and I was going to figure out a way to make my pseudophilosophy into a reality again. It took a while to come up with the words, but as they started to roll off the tongue and I translated them to Calibri, size 12, 1.5-spaced, Chase called.

"Hey. I don't know what you had planned for the weekend, but I want to do something."

She said it with the ironic precision so contrary to my realization that one would only find in a fiction book or a television sitcom.

"My plans are always subject to change, what do you have in mind?" It was a lie in that something that doesn't exist cannot change.

"I want to try skydiving."

This is a decent time for an aside about my fear of heights. I fucking hate heights. I do not know what it is, but if I had to sit and think about it, this is what I would say:

I believe in the weight of words insofar as one can use them. I do not think that there are long-term effects for nearly everything. Barring obvious exceptions, people move on from sexual experiences, people can also move on emotionally, and in a 4-dimensional reality (if you think there are more you are most likely friendless and I don't care that you believe I am wrong) time inevitably moves all things along. When it comes to tattoos that is not the case. They are always there as reminders of that moment in time. With heights, it is even more permanent that a misstep or a malfunction is fatal. 30 feet or 3000 feet (or however far up it is), it is irrelevant, I don't do heights.

The plan instantly became diversion.

"I was thinking a trip out of town." I was willing to go far.

"Well, that's the best part. The closest place to skydive is like 3 hours away. That way we get a road trip, like you want, and we can skydive, like I want."

What the fuck? Something out there was stacked very seriously against me.

"I have to think about it."

"Is something the matter?"

"Yeah."

Shit. Shit. Shit. What? I had nothing.

"Awe, baby, if something is wrong we need to be able to talk about it."

"My aunt died in a skydiving accident."

This was not a new low for me, but a newish low. I wasn't much of a flagrant liar. Until I was backed into a corner.

"My mother would have a heart attack if I did something like that."

"Oh, wow. I'm sorry. I am really sorry, Tristan. I never knew."

I didn't either, until now.

"Well, why don't you come on over when you can and we will figure it out."

There was much to figure out, but I had to do most of it sans the lady.

"I will come over in a couple of hours, sounds good?"

"Yep."

"Great. I'll see you soon, babe."

"Bye, T."

Okay, now I had a couple of hours to think and figure out. I sat in this coffee shop looking at people and wondering what they were doing with their lives. I got online and looked up that dude who did the NPR interview. I couldn't remember his name at first but it only took about eleven seconds online to find one of the most famous people within his own niche.

I perused his site and it was the typical life coach rigma-role: Power words, exercise, mindset, testimonials etc. I didn't like the design. I didn't like the fake layer on top of life. It was prozakian (I know Prozac is spelled with a 'c', but my neolo-gism looks 30 times better with a 'k'). Everyone seemed delud-ed. They all somehow made more money after spending $75 an hour talking to his 'certified' wellness coaches.

I didn't buy it. I wanted to, I wanted to buy it and see the connection. And I wanted to pick a path and go down it. I just didn't understand how people didn't see through this shit.

I leaned back and rubbed my eyes. The computer screen does wonders to the eyes and after straining my vision staring at essays earlier, and straining my faith in humanity grading said essays, this guy's website was the icing on the cake. I watched people around me a little more. I still felt directionless, but be-came pissed off sitting there, unable to understand why.

A couple of people talking caught my attention. They were talking about some current event that I didn't know any-thing about. One reiterated what he heard from a talking head on a news network and the other rebutted a tagline that he had to have derived from another network based on the fact that they disagreed. It went on, my patience for the conversation, that is, for a few minutes.

I couldn't believe how fucking ignorant they sounded. I know most people talk this way in what they would call intel-ligent conversation, but it never ceases to amaze me that this is how 'educated' people function. It instantly called to mind about 300 class discussions I have been a part of since I entered the university system. I looked at what was on my computer screen. A picture of a way-too-happy guy in a suit with his testi-monial about how a wellness coach changed the game for him.

And that was when it clicked for me.

CHAPTER 31

Questions

There are too many answers and conclusions already out there, so don't ask too many questions. They will bury and consume you. The decisive man may not even have a trajectory, but a direction or a speed is usually adequate to keep up the appearance of someone who has his shit together, which is a prerequisite to getting what you want from people who want to be like that. Or even people who don't want to be like that but who naturally capitulate to the stronger will.

The stronger will always win.

The coffee to go on my way out was a great idea. It was a cold day and it kept my hands warm walking 60 feet to my car, and then after my thirteen minute drive the additional 40 or 50 feet to Chase's from my parking spot in her complex. I didn't drink much of it once I got to her apartment, but it is always worth the buck-fifty to have it handy if I do want it. I don't mind cold coffee so the option doesn't go out the window for quite a while.

"So skydiving is out of the question?" she asked.

"Do you know how cold it is?"

"Yeah, I didn't think that mattered."

"I thought nerds were more scientific."

"What?" She didn't take that one well.

"It's colder at higher altitudes. If it's 50 here, it's 30 in the sky, or colder."

"I'm sorry I didn't study meteorology."

"That's okay. That's why you have a boyfriend who knows everything."

"Except that *tsatiki* is Greek."

"Italian is practically Greek." I was very wrong about that argument a week or so prior.

"What should we do then?"

What happened next was foregone. It lasted about two hours and took place on the sofa, her coffee table, the floor in the TV room and the kitchen counter (just for kicks). It reaffirmed my belief that I am the best lover in this country. We were naked on her couch not really talking when she asked again about what I want to do this weekend. Maybe she asked that every weekend but it was a motif that I couldn't shake. I couldn't not think it had more meaning than what she actually wanted to do this weekend. It was a metaphor every time I thought about it. It meant my master plan.

I hate that 'the master plan' sounds Naziistic. It sounds like a wing in the Holocaust museum. It is what it is, and if I could ever think of another way to put it, I would. But I also thought it sounded bold and worthy of my genius. The Master Plan is God's will. It is all encompassing and it applies to everything. Unfortunately it didn't exist much like the Christian Master Plan, and the God that people associate with it. I was thinking too deeply about this, because Chase interrupted my staring at the floor.

"Hey, any ideas?"

"Nope."

"Dinner tonight?"

"Absolutely."

"Let's watch a movie."

Then came that look that I wasn't going to get a pick in what the movie was. I would regret watching it, and I would regret the aftermath of not watching it. There needed to be a concession, but I didn't yet know what.

Anal maybe? That is a great deterrent, but also worth dying inside for a couple of hours watching Tom Hanks and Meg Ryan fall in love on screen.

Probably not worth asking.

"For being so cool, you have the worst taste in movies." I said it with a straight face. She hit me with a pillow and we left it at that.

We didn't arrive at any conclusions, but figured a nice dinner was in order. I recommended Andolinni's and she said no. I know why. I wanted to push it. I don't know why I did, but I did. Amazingly, that never happened. We settled on pizza (gourmet pizza), and she picked a movie that wasn't going to drive me to suicide. The night turned out to be okay. She was still fun, and was debunking my belief that couples lose interest after a short period of time. I thought as long as things persisted, I would be a happy guy. She was great in bed, smart, gorgeous and really liked me too. We were happy. . .*We were happy as a unit.*

I, personally, felt like something was missing. I was starting to fill in the gaps, but the big picture continued to elude me.

The credits rolled and I took our empty pizza box (gourmet pizza box) to the kitchen. We overdid it on dinner and I was fighting to stay awake, but as we moved to the bedroom to sleep, I became restless. I spent a good deal of the movie thinking about the people on that website. I thought about those dumbasses assessing the world situation over coffee and I thought about how all of this tied together. I laid down on my back and she was on my chest, but I couldn't fall asleep. She wasn't completely out yet and I moved her to get up.

"What are you doing?" she was groggy and I barely understood her.

"I need water."

I paced in her kitchen completely naked, sipping on water from a cup with two cartoon frogs on it. It was lame but enduring, in a Chase way.

What do I want to do? What the fuck am I going to do when I graduate? Why can I not make a decision to save my life?

I asked "Why" and "What" too many times without an-

swers. I was getting nowhere pacing around asking myself questions. I didn't get anything out of it since finding out about Ash,
which I eventually came to terms with. I kept pacing and asking myself these open-ended questions, but I knew it was going
nowhere. Her floor was cold. I went into her room and put my
socks on. I thought about staying and pacing until I came to a
conclusion, but I decided to go home.

She woke up as I was putting my pants on and she asked
what I was doing.

"I gotta go home, babe. I have some things to take care
of."

"No, come back to bed. It's warm." That was her logic
at the time, and it was one of the few logical arguments I ever
heard from a girl that I was with. It didn't work.

"I want to, but this is going to drive me crazy if I don't
take care of it."

"It's midnight. Do it in the morning." She said into her
pillow, eyes shut. Still groggy.

"It's about 1:30, but I will come by in the morning, K?"

"Hmmm." I think that meant, "Okay, go ahead". So I finished dressing, kissed her on the exposed shoulder and went out
to the car. It was fucking cold outside and it hit me the second I
opened her door. I was awake from thinking at a million miles
an hour, but this sealed the deal. I was primed.

I didn't listen to music on the way home. It was silent,
dark and in the glow of my dashboard, very pensive. When I
passed the drugstore that I stopped at the other night I saw the
cop in the parking lot. I waved. He probably didn't see me in
the dark, but I considered him a Samaritan, and he warranted
a wave.

I stopped my car when I got home and sat in it for ten
minutes. I was out of questions. Rather, I was at a loss for the
right questions, but I knew something would come. It was going
to be a mental war of attrition.

I must have used up everything I had because the moment I got inside I became tired. I made a cup of tea to fight it

and fell asleep while it steeped.

***

I woke up on my couch at 7am. It was a good start to the day, but off of maybe five hours of sleep. The first thing I did was brush my teeth and assess where I was at. The tea on the counter had to go, but I quickly replaced it with a fresh cup and sat on the couch, still wearing the clothes I wore the night before. I needed to finish grading those essays and check that off of my list. I thought that lightning might strike twice so I decided to take them to the coffee shop I was at the day before. It was good for my thought process.

Showered and shaved, I went with the essays in tow and sat at the table I had yesterday. I felt fresh and knocked out a significant number of papers as the morning wore on. I didn't think much about anything, but it was edifying that this shit job was winding to a close. I took a break and just listened to the bustle of a Saturday morning. The caffeinated people chatted and recuperated from their Friday night. They enjoyed the day off of their banal adulthoods. Some read newspapers and filled their heads with new opinions about the functionality of the world machine.

Nothing too profound happened. I did finish grading the essays, and I wanted to sit around and people watch, but my last nerve was raw. I couldn't decide what to do at the moment, but it was something kinetic. I needed to move around. Academics make me ashamed for people who claim to be so smart, but are so incapable of anything but arguing and writing their obscure and pointless views. A true measure of intelligence would be something like envisioning perfection and achieving it. Something like what I had given up. For now.

CHAPTER 32

"Tristan, it's me, Mrs. Daily. You never came by and I tried calling twice. I can imagine you are busy, but not fulfilling your obligations in the first place is why you were originally on academic probation. I talked to Professor Sandoval and he hadn't heard from you in a few days either. If something is wrong, you know where you can go."

I truly hated her. I threw my phone into the backseat after listening to the message I missed from her yesterday. I didn't even think about that appointment, but now I was glad that I didn't go. I was back on track anyhow, so pissing myself off talking to that fuck would have just ruined my Friday, which was not too bad.

I still didn't have the slightest inkling as to what I was going to do next year, but I think I knew where to go. It pained me that I was essentially set up to get a job and I think the economics of it were that Chase and I would eventually move in together. All of this stuff sounded like it was in the bag, but I didn't like it. I didn't want it. Maybe I did. I don't know. Who knows what they want at that age?

I sat in my car for a minute looking for a CD to listen to for the ten-minute commute back to campus. I settled on one and began driving.

When I was in student council in high school, we had a meeting after a school shooting cost about six students their lives. It was in another state and in another demographic, but we were obligated to put our young minds together and figure it out at the behest of Coach. . . Carpenter, I think his name was. It didn't matter now, but something he said always stuck with me. He said that maybe those kids just did it. Maybe something deep inside just snapped. He said that when he drove down the freeway by himself that he always wanted to do an E-brake turn. He said that he never did it, and that he probably never would, but that it was something in him that he couldn't explain.

I didn't pull my E-brake on the way home, but when I parked and actuated it I thought of what he said.

Rather than go home I took all of the papers in my car to Sandoval's office. He wasn't there, but as a director of a department he had an inbox that was more than adequate. I put a sticky note, compliments of his secretary's desk, on the stack of papers.

> *I will never grade another paper again. Thank you for the opportunity to figure that out.*
> *Tristan*

I knew he wouldn't take it personally. It was like I had just cut a cancer out of my life. It would be an exaggeration to say that there were no words to describe how I felt getting rid of those fucking things, but at the very least, I would need a thesaurus to find one that was good enough.

I went home and looked at that guy's website again. I couldn't explain why it was so compelling to me. I didn't agree with so much of it. I didn't think much of it at all, but there was this magnetism to me about the. . .I don't know what. I stared at Jane, a mother of two and small business owner who has 'never been happier' thanks to blah blah blah.

I thought again about those two assholes saying (and believing) what they heard on the news. I looked at Jane's fake smile. I looked at the color scheme of the webpage. I looked at my manuscript. I smiled, because I got it.

My inbox had nothing new. Namely, nothing from Josh. It had been a day and I figured by Saturday afternoon that he wasn't going to work over the weekend. It was okay. I sent him an affirmation that this book was going to happen. There was nothing I could do but wait. At least, as far as the book was concerned. I never deleted emails, I just foldered them. I don't know if that is not a word, but I think it's obvious enough. I never did it to emails from potential clients. I just left them there. I had about twenty of them and I started to re-read them.

My mood was good. I didn't have a Master Plan. I think it was out there, though, somewhere in the cold autumn air. I remembered that my phone was in the backseat of my car and I wanted to do something. I had a few hours of daylight left and I knew Chase wanted to get together. I promised her while she was asleep the night before that I would go over in the morning. I was only about seven hours late, but she never called so I wasn't too worried about it.

"Hey, where were you?" (Do I need to explain that I got my cell and called her?)

"Finishing up some work. Can you do something right now?"

"Yeah, I kept my weekend free for you. I am home now." She sounded vindictive, but I was not going to let her play games.

"I'll be over soon."

"Okay."

Yeah, she was definitely vindictive. I tried not to think about it so that I wouldn't get worked up and contentious on my drive over. Instead, I drove slow and enjoyed the sweet release of those chains I accepted from Sandoval. I thought about Jane, and Tom, and Brad, and the nine other toothy smiles, short bios and adjectivy synopses of their success. So much success. So much inspiration.

When I arrived, she was all smiles. I didn't trust that her tone changed so much from the phone to her doorstep. Maybe I was just overthinking it. Small talk, kisses and questions about my day. It was so domestic. It was plain and I got uneasy. She wanted to. . .that's right, watch another movie. Yay. She had a menu for Chinese takeout and we opted for delivery. My jewism comment about their delivery charge didn't get the laugh that I expected. But that was the only real unease that we experienced. At that moment.

Over our sweet and sour MSG and pork fried MSG, with some garbage love story in the background, I brought up my book.

"Why would you do that?" Her question was too pointed. To me it was obvious that I would do what I wanted, and to her it was obvious that I should absolutely not do so. I didn't know if she was just being contrary or if she really didn't like the idea, so I dropped it and kept 'watching' the film.

About three minutes later, she brought it up again. "Why don't you write another book?"

"Have you ever written a book, Chase? It is not just something that I can do in a weekend. I'm not going to start over because you don't like it."

"Me? It's not about me. Why don't you ask Ashton's family about your book?" It was Ashleigh, but that's not the point. Why would she bring that up?

I mumbled "Too soon" over a bite of rice and tried again to drop it. I don't argue with girls. I just don't.

"You didn't learn anything from that, did you?"

What the fuck was she getting at?

"I didn't *learn anything* from that? Are you shitting me?" Now I was mad. "You were the one who said that everything was his fucking choice. Don't just decide that I am instantly culpable because you don't like what I do."

"I thought you stopped."

Okay, I had stopped. But she said it like I was a reformed junky.

"I don't think you completely understand."

"Don't patronize me, Tristan. Are you doing it or not?"

"Publishing? Yes. Why is it so horrid that I want to do this?"

"Why can't you just write something else if you want to publish?" She inflected the word to make it sound like it was a crime.

"Chase, I don't like the way you hold your chopsticks." I learned this one from Stevo, who I hadn't spoken to in quite a while. I needed to call him.

"What does that have to do with anything?"

It was too simple. I was not going to get anywhere with this argument, so I was throwing the match. I was using a woman's best tool for arguing against her. Illogicalness. I don't know if that is a word either, but 'illogicalism' sounds wrong as fuck.

She was pissed, but didn't have a response. She said something under her breath. I didn't follow it up and we sat there in silence not really watching the movie.

There was tension, then she moved in closer. There was less tension and she moved closer yet. Her body language said "forgiveness". I accepted it as though it was an apology, and everything was okay within twenty minutes. Everything except for the fact that on a Saturday night I was watching some shit movie that could not even mirror real dialogue.

"Tristan?"

"Let's not talk about it."

"Hummm, I, I love you."

Wow, okay. Now I really don't want to talk about it.

CHAPTER 33

I broke up with Chase. It is significant enough to my story to recount here, that night, over Chinese food and one of her favorite movies:

"Humm, I, I love you."

Silence (for about eleven seconds). . .

"Chase,"

"Yeah?"

"I want to break up."

Tears.

I was hurt inside, but did well not to show it. I took a fortune cookie when I left, as we had not opened them yet, and ate it in the car. It read, "You are bold." I knew that what I had done was the right thing. And it was reaffirmed by thousands of years of Chinese philosophy.

I heard back from Josh Diggins on a Monday and he told me that the book had to be either more tongue-in-cheek, or slightly more politically correct. Meaning any trace of politically correct would suffice. I went with tongue-in-cheek and was working on a preface after the 7,000 edits and tweaks had been made. Publishing alone was a reward *per se*. I thought about it more in terms of a self-contained resume. It was an accomplishment that would be written under my name, on *my* webpage, along with some skewed statistics about the number of people I helped, and some other trivialities that were going to make the picture of me more complete. It was going to be accompanied by testimonials, million-dollar smiles, pictures and different fonts to emphasize the gamut of feel good moods that I have bestowed on the world.

While I sat at my computer with the monumental task of self-editing for the fifth time, albeit with more direction, I stopped to think about how great I was and how good it felt to be where I was in life. I earned this.

My phone rang and I assumed it was Chase, but it was my 'counselor'. I was happy to answer.

"This is Tristan." I know people don't answer their phones like that, but I did, that time. There was a pause because I don't think she expected that one.

"Hey, Tristan, how are you?" Before she gave me time to answer: "This is Mrs. Daily. You missed our little appointment last week."

I sat quiet, with the intention of her having to follow up her own statements, and not elicit some apology from me. It worked, because after about five seconds of silence she continued:

"So do you think there is going to be a time today that you could drop by?"

By now, she was on speaker and I was typing a response to Josh.

"How is Tuesday?"

"That sounds okay, how about after lunch? I have other students in the morning."

"How about it? Two?"

"Okay, Tristan, don't forget this time, okay?"

I just hung up. I had no reason to pander to her. I hated everything she stood for and was working on my attempt at creating a life for myself and others that ran so contrary to her situation.

I thought back to my last realization. When I sat there listening to those two guys at the coffee shop, it occurred to me that I was going to spend a lifetime trying to change the game from the outside. I wanted to invent something new and expected people to come flocking over. What snapped inside of me, what I knew instantly about my approach that was flawed was that so many people are too deep into what is already there. They are bogged down in their dogmas and beliefs and if there was one way to get to them, it was going to be at their level.

Chase would have been a great addition to the picture that I wanted to paint, but she didn't want to be in it. She had her own picture that I was supposed to fit in by some means of transfiguration. Something that I deleted from the original copy of my book that was going to make it into the final copy was a brief section on every girl's desire to find a broken guy and fix him. I took it out because it was not congruous with the message I wanted to send about the projection of having one's shit together, but I learned that it was so real and so applicable that it would be the perfect tool for anyone who wanted to use it. Also, people with their shit together don't buy books on how to do so. Maybe this can be an earlier chapter to give early advice on working with what you've got. I think it all sounded good. I felt like myself again.

There were a few more things I had to do, but after sending a blanket email to all of the people who asked for my services telling them that I have some time after finals, there was one thing left to do to really kick-off this new era in my life.

It was not hard to convince Jeremy to get lunch. I needed the break from staring at the computer and he surely needed a break from doing whatever he was doing. I'm almost certain it was lame. I innocently recommended empanadas and he jumped on the chance to meet up. He agreed before I finished my sentence. Maybe he really wanted Cuban. I knew that was exactly what I wanted.

I saved everything on my computer, then emailed it to myself just in case something happened to the hard drive. I saw it in a movie and I have copied almost every addition to the book since then. By now there must have been 100 different versions and revisions to the book, all stored online. It has never really come in handy, but I know I am going to fuck myself the day I delete anything.

I don't normally dress to the nines to get Cuban. I normally don't do anything. I didn't think it even warranted a shower to meet Jeremy for lunch, but I was trying with all of my might to get over the last vestiges of lethargy from the last couple of months, including the complacency that I felt with Chase. I called it comfort when we were together.

I hadn't noticed this before, but since we started dating I gained a few pounds. Maybe this shower was a good idea. What else was wrong with me? I checked for lumps the best I could remember from Sex Ed. Nothing out of the ordinary. I did need a trim. Badly. I looked at myself naked as the shower warmed up. I looked in the mirror at my posture. It had also suffered a little bit. I speculated that so much time on the couch watching so many movies had done that to me. That was all a thing of the past. It was time to look forward again.

It didn't take long to dress and look my best. I had all of the makings for it, but it was a matter of just putting things on. I included some cologne that I hadn't worn much of lately. I didn't factor in how cold it was outside and after opening my door I promptly shut it and tried something different. Something that included a scarf.

Now I was ready. I thought of how Chase would adjust my scarf every time I put it on. I went to my car and even though it never works at first I turned the heat all the way up and sat for three minutes while cold air issued from the vents. When it finally warmed up a bit I drove the short drive to lunch and, as usual, Jeremy was already there.

"Hey, friend."

"Hey, I'm glad you called, Amber and I were arguing about baby names."

"Is she pregnant?"

"No, that's the bitch of it. She isn't, but we are fighting over the stupidest shit and after we run out of that, we can't even agree on something that doesn't even affect us yet."

"Wow, you are a lucky bastard." I was trying to contain my jealousy, but I don't think it required much effort.

"Everything is fine, but we don't agree on almost anything."

"Then why are you even together?"

"Because, dude, they are just baby names." It clicked. I don't know if he had a shred of dignity left, but I sat back and looked at my friend. I was happy for him. I was happy that he was happy. I was happy that I had just dodged that bullet.

Out of the back of the restaurant came my motive. She was wearing a tight black shirt. Jeremy did something right and actually seated himself in her section, not that I think anyone else was even serving today.

We ate and shot the shit for a while. I felt good. I was full. I felt like a cocked handgun ready to fire. While Jeremy talked about baby names trying to convince himself that he was right, I drifted off and wondered why I never did this stuff for girls. I think I could use what I know about them to their advantage. So many showed up to school and had no direction. Maybe I needed a few 'Janes' like that one guy had. I was bending over backwards trying to help nerds get laid while half of the campus had problems looking for nice guys, like those I helped. I don't know why I didn't think of this before, but it was going to be good. Or a disaster. I was excited about the prospect either way.

I didn't say anything about Chase. I didn't want to talk about it. I didn't want to think about it. This was exactly the reason that I didn't date. I hated how it felt, so I did what I could not to think about it. And just like that I got my chance not to think about it. Jeremy excused himself to the little boy's room and she walked over in unison with his departure.

And so I decided to bring in the new era with a bang:

"Do you want a refill on your tea?" She was one of the hottest girls in this town and I had never had this chance in my life. Something had always gotten in the way before, but the stars lined up perfectly and we were the only two people on earth at that moment.

"Do you want to get together sometime?"

She looked at me blankly. The anticipation was broken after a few seconds when she took my cup and walked away. I sat there, staring in amazement. She didn't even say no.

Jeremy came back. She set the check in front of him without even looking at me.

"What did I miss?"

"Nothing, man. Do you want to meet up at Andolinni's later this week?"

There was a girl named Sara that I had to go get. Maybe I would find that good addition to my picture after all.

www.ingramcontent.com/pod-product-compliance
Lightning Source LLC
Chambersburg PA
CBHW060933180626
46817CB00004B/1519